WHEELS

OF

BETRAYAL

Book 3: Coyote Ridge Penitentiary.

An Outlaw Biker Tale

ALEX MCRAE

Published by Iron Battalion Press

Made in the USA 2026

Wheels of Betrayal. Book 3: Coyote Ridge Penitentiary. An Outlaw Biker Tale is a work of fiction. Names, places, and incidents are products of the Author's imagination, or are used fictitiously. Any resemblance to actual events, locales, or persons living or dead is purely coincidental.

Twitter : @AlexMcRae99

Instagram: @alexmcrae99

Amazon:
https://www.amazon.com/stores/AlexMcRae/author/B0F344WTHB

Wheels of Betrayal: Coyote Ridge Penitentiary: An Outlaw Biker Tale Book 3

Hi there. My name is Ian Harrison, and I am a journalism student at ASU here in Phoenix. One of my final-year assignments was to interview a controversial figure and gather their life story. I chose to interview infamous outlaw biker Jack “Razor” Sullivan. I don't know why. I guess I have always been kind of obsessed with outlaw bikers and motorcycle clubs. So last month, I spoke with Jack “Razor” Sullivan about growing up and riding around the New York City motorcycle club scene in the 1980s and 1990s.

On my second day of interviewing Razor, he talked about his life in Arizona back in the spring of 2000. This is my third and final interview with him.

I hope you enjoy it.

Ian Harrison, Arizona, June 2025.

Chapter One

Twenty years in prison. That's what I was facing if Agent Sanders didn't come through for me. You see, for the last four years, I had been working as a Confidential Informant for the Bureau of Enforcement for Substances, Arms, and Contraband (BESAC), helping them put bad guys behind bars. I had been caught up in a raid gone wrong, and now I was facing twenty years in prison. My handler, Agent Sanders, had been in Washington, D.C., during the raid, and I was confident that, as soon as the trial he was testifying in was over, he would be back and sort this mess out. All I had to do was stay alive until then.

I was sent to Coyote Ridge Penitentiary. The locals called it "The Ridge." Perched on the edge of the blistering Sonoran Desert, it was a crumbling fortress of steel, concrete, and dust. Built in 1936 and barely updated since, it was surrounded by rusting barbed wire and sun-baked guard towers. The Ridge was originally a territorial prison and still reeked of chain-gang sweat and bad blood. Its stone-walled cell blocks trap summer heat like an oven, and in winter, the chill bites through every crack in the mortar.

The prison's yard is little more than a dirt lot scorched by the sun, where lifers and outlaws sort themselves into tribes, watched by indifferent guards in mirrored sunglasses who would just as quickly shoot you if you disobeyed a command. Stories say the solitary wing known as "The Pit" still holds the ghosts of men who died screaming back in the 1950s, when discipline meant fists, boots, and broom handles.

Officially, Coyote Ridge is a high-security facility, but anyone who's done time there knows the gangs and the guards write the rules; they just try to keep the body count low. It was a place where justice ends at the gate, a man's only currency is fear, loyalty, and how far he's willing to go to survive.

All I had to do was keep my head down and stay alive until Sanders returned from Washington, D.C.

Chapter Two

My first week, I was pretty much kept in a solitary cell. I guess they call it the "intake" part of the prison. I'm not afraid to admit it, but I was scared. I had heard stories of guys slashing their wrists in their first few days; they would rather die than go into the mainline population. My concern with something like that was: you slash your wrists, or your neck, or wherever, and then you survive. Congrats, now you are in prison, on the yard, in a weakened capacity. Not advisable.

I wasn't particularly scared of fighting someone, even a bigger guy. Actually, in my experience, guys who were bigger than most people, say, from their early teens, were usually not good fighters. Many (not all) of them had used their size to intimidate most of their lives and therefore never bothered to learn to fight. That said, if you did fight a bigger enemy who did know how to fight, they did gas out very quickly. Of course, if one of their punches connected right away, forget it. You were going into a coma or going to get a broken jaw.

Smaller guys: their punches didn't hurt as much, but most of them had much better stamina than bigger guys and could whale on you for a while before they got exhausted. Anyone who has ever knocked someone out knows that if you hit the jaw in the right place, even with a so-so punch, you can take someone out. There is a nerve between the skull and the jawbone that is almost like a "computer restart" button. You hit it just right, lights out. You are going bye-bye time.

So yeah, fighting didn't bother me. I was happy to fight you in prison. I mean, think about it. What's the worst they can do? Lock you up? You're already in prison! What concerned me, though, were sneak attacks. It takes balls to square up to someone and know you might get beaten; you might be the one doing the beating. Sneak attacks, someone comes up behind you with a makeshift weapon and shanks you repeatedly. How can you defend against that? A guy can be skinnier, smaller, with no fight skills. They can still stick you and take you out. That's what concerned me.

The week was spent with medical tests and psychological tests. Do you have AIDS? Have you ever been a member of a street gang? Are you thinking about self-harming? I am sure most men thought about "self-harming" when they were faced with twenty years in one of the worst penitentiaries in the state. No, scratch that. Definitely the worst penitentiary in the state. What person would not be thinking of a way to get out of this shithole?

I asked a couple of the guards to make a phone call. I was keen to get hold of Agent Sanders and start the process of getting out of here. I figured once he was back in Phoenix, there was probably a process he had to go through to get me out. That could take a week or so. Better to start now. Every time I called, I got the runaround: "Not back yet," "Yes, I will pass on your message," "Yes, I gave his office your last message," and on and on. Very frustrating.

After a week on the "intake" yard, I was told I was being transferred to gen pop. I guess they figured I was not in any danger of self-harm and knew where to put me. I ended up being sent to D-wing, which was the home of convicted murderers and, I guess, manslaughter offenders. Is there a word for people who accidentally kill someone? You know, like if you murder someone, you are a murderer. So if you "manslaughter" someone, what does that make you? A manslaughterer? Anyway, I digress. I was transferred to D-wing with the rest of "my kind," according to a prison guard called Briggs.

I was taken in at night. D-wing was the old-school, traditional-style prison wing: three tiers of cells on one wall, with a guard walkway on the opposite side of the building. On the ground floor, there were built-in tables and seating for prisoners to play cards, read books, socialize, whatever. I was taken to the top tier (third floor). I noticed there were steel grills welded to the balcony railings. I assumed they were there to stop prisoners from throwing their buddies off the top floors, or maybe someone had tried to kill themselves by leaping off, hence the addition of the grills.

My cell was on the third floor. I felt a bunch of eyes on me as I was escorted down the corridor. I knew enough about prison etiquette not to look into the other cells as I passed by. That would be considered damn rude, and I didn't want to piss off anybody, especially not in my first twenty-four hours on the block.

It was like a jail cell out of the movies: two steel bunks on the left-hand side with a paper-thin mattress, if you could call it that. I have had friends with foam mats under their sleeping bags while camping that were thicker than these mattresses. A sink/washbasin combo, and in the back, a toilet bowl with no seat or cover. I would guess the cell was about eight ft deep and slightly wider than six ft all the way to the wall. If I stood in the middle and stretched both my arms out, I could almost touch either side of the cell. Despite having two bunks, I was there on my own, grateful that I did not have to share, at least for now. I am sure they would eventually throw someone else into the cell with me.

There was some shelving for personal belongings, but not much. Like, I guess a change of clothes, socks, underwear, a toothbrush, shaving cream, a razor, and that's about it. There was a heavy woollen blanket on the bed and a lumpy pillow.

The guards undid my chains and had me step back while one of them shouted to close my cell door. I rubbed my wrists and ankles to help get my circulation going again and took stock of my situation. Ideally, I would be here for a week or two, then back out into the free world. Even one night in here was one night too many. Hurry up, Agent Sanders.

I slept like, eh. Well, not terribly, but not great either. I guess then I slept better than expected. All night long, I could hear men snoring, sobbing, farting, you name it, I could hear it. I figured out fast enough that sound travels in a place like this. At 5:30 am, the lights came on, and you could almost hear the place come alive with activity as prisoners readied themselves to be let out to start their day. First port of call would be breakfast.

I jumped up, took a piss, washed my face, brushed my teeth, and got dressed. As I was pulling on my cheap slip-on sneakers, one of the guards walked by, shouting for us to get up and be ready. Five minutes later, I heard him shout again as the cell door swung open, and we were told to line up by our doors. As I stepped onto the balcony, I felt every eye in the place on me.

I followed the guys as we turned left and headed down the stairs. I had no clue where we were headed, just that we were going for breakfast. I was starving. I knew the food was probably going to be bad, but when you're hungry, you're grateful for any form of sustenance, good or lousy. We joined the men from the second tier and the ground floor and were led out of a door on the opposite side from where I had come in the night before. We walked down a long, sterile corridor and were then led into what you would call the food hall. I could smell coffee and warm food from across the room.

I joined my place in line with the other dudes from the third tier. I needed to figure out the lay of the land, or should I say, the politics of this prison, fast.

I was standing in line and minding my own business when a hand grabbed my shoulder, and someone swung me around. I am usually hyper-aware of my surroundings, but whoever this person was caught me off guard. I didn't hear them approach at all.

"Get out of my way, PUNK," the stranger shouted at me.

Sizing him up, the dude was about 22 years old, six feet tall, and fairly solid. I knew enough about prison politics that if someone called you a punk, you had to hit him immediately. So that's what I did. I hit him with a right hook across his jaw. I don't think he was expecting it, and he was definitely rocked. The guys from my tier stepped back to let us fight.

The stranger lunged at me. I stepped to one side, and he slipped as he missed me. I saw my chance and kneed him right in his back. I could hear him gasp as the air got knocked out of his lungs. He recovered quickly and twisted to try to get back to his feet. I used my right forearm like an iron bar to whack him across his neck. I was winning. Well, I was winning until I felt a crack across the back of my head. I assumed one of his buddies had joined in to back him up. I turned to swing on my new opponent and was met with another crack across my face from one of the guards. I was literally seeing stars. If you ever watched the 1960s Batman TV show, you might remember the comic-book-style fight scenes, the ones where cartoon flashes would say things like "Oof" and "Boom." That was literally what I was seeing as this goon beat me down. I was rocked and fell to the floor. I recall hearing a bunch of prisoners cheering. The last thing I remember was being dragged off by two guards. My only consolation was that the younger guy who attacked me was also getting dragged away.

So much for breakfast.

Chapter Three

I woke up bloodied and bruised in a cell. Coming to my senses, I realized this was not the cell I had just been given. This was something different. No bed, just a shitter. No bars on the door, just a solid steel door with a hatch. As my scrambled brain tried to piece together what had happened, it slowly began to come back to me.

I was standing in line for food. Some dude had come up and attacked me. I beat him down. The guards had dragged me off for fighting. They beat me down, two dudes with billy clubs wailing on me. From what I could remember, their main beef was, "They ran the joint, not me." They got me good: split lip, bit my damn tongue, probably a chipped tooth or two, a couple of cracked ribs, bruising over both my legs and my back. Looking back on that incident now, I see their logic. They didn't care if we prisoners beat the shit out of each other. Actually, they probably preferred that. As long as we were beefing with each other, we had no energy to beef with them.

My theory is that the real reason they beat me down is that they saw me as a threat. How do I explain it? "Like, don't get any ideas of turning on us, boy." I guess it was somewhat akin to puppy training. They beat you enough, and you begin to learn who the "master" is. Fuck that. I would never bow to those losers. If anything, that made me more determined to never kowtow to them. Fuckers.

Now what? I was stripped down to my boxers in an empty cell. Was I going to get any breakfast? I doubt it. Shit. How long had I been out for? Not sure about you, but getting knocked out is weird. You can get knocked out, have epic dreams that last hours and hours, only to be revived and find out you were out for 45 seconds. You can get knocked out, it feels like a minute, and you have been out for two whole days. Like I said, weird.

There was only artificial light coming into my cell. No windows, and I couldn't see out of the steel door. Was it still daytime? Was it nighttime? Was it even the same day? I really didn't know. I tried to get up to piss, but my legs hurt. Sheesh, my whole body hurts. I staggered to my feet and made my way to the pisser. It was an effort to piss, but I finally made it happen.

It made me realize I was thirsty. So thirsty. I needed water. I tried to remember survival training from high school. What was it? Three minutes without air? Three days without water? Thirty days without food? I dunno, something like that. I needed a drink. Could they even hold me here without providing water? I had no clue what my rights were.

I sat back down in the corner of the cell. Now what? I tell you, one thing no one warns you about before going to prison is the boredom. Like, everyone knows about the fighting, the stabbings, the extreme violence, but the boredom was the real killer. I was so bored. Bored to tears. At least in school, when I was bored, I could stare out the window or admire the hot chicks. Here, there was nothing. Gimme something to read, a newspaper, a magazine, something. I would settle for reading the Bible at this point.

I contemplated working out, but my body was so battered at this point that I would probably do myself more damage than good. I think I fell back to sleep at one point. The clang of steel woke me up. My door! I sat up right away, keen to see daylight and maybe even speak to someone. No luck. A slot opened at the bottom of my cell, and a tray slid through.

"Hey," I whispered, "what time is it?"

"Five" a voice replied.

"Day or night?" I asked.

"What the fuck? Night, dumbass," said the voice.

"What day?" I asked.

Before the voice had a chance to reply, I heard another voice.

"No talking. Move along."

The slot closed up. I could hear them bolting the door on the other side. That must have been the guard. I would have traded anything right now to be on the other side of this door.

I examined the tray. I had a bologna sandwich on white bread, a banana, and a juice box. Too bad if you were a vegan. I guess you would eat the bread and the banana.

I grabbed the juice box and popped the provided straw through the top. My mouth was so dry. I drank half and saved the rest. Who was to say how long it would be before I got another beverage?

I ate the sandwich, then the banana. I tell you, right then and there, that was the best-tasting sandwich I had ever had. I had to eat on the right side of my mouth, as my left lip was still swollen from the beating I had taken.

After eating, I sat back in the corner of my cell and contemplated my life. How did it end up like this? All I wanted to do was ride motorcycles and be free. This was as far from freedom as it gets. No scoot, no open road, no nothing. I had to get hold of Sanders and get out of this shitbox.

Chapter Four

I must have passed out again. The next thing I knew, I was being woken up by the clang of steel again. The food hatch! Had twenty-four hours passed already? Had I been asleep that long?

"Pass the old tray back," the voice said. It was hard to tell, but it sounded like the same voice from yesterday.

I slid the tray towards the gap. A hand grabbed it, and moments later, another tray appeared in its place. Another sandwich. An apple and a small carton of milk.

"Thanks," I said. "What time is it?"

"Five," the voice said.

So I had been out for twenty-four hours?

"p.m., right?" I asked.

"No. Five in the morning, dumbass," snapped the voice. It was hard to tell whether they were being sarcastic. I guessed I'd figure it out at some point during the day.

The sandwich was either turkey or chicken (I couldn't tell). A strange way to start breakfast, if my friend outside doing deliveries was indeed telling the truth. The apple and the milk were a nice touch. In solitary confinement, having no toothbrush, the apple at least helped my teeth feel somewhat clean. I couldn't recall the last time I drank milk (other than in my morning coffee), maybe at age ten or twelve. Weird, but a welcome relief from the juice box.

I still had no idea how many days I had been in solitary, but my body was starting to heal somewhat from the brutal beating I had received from the guards. I decided to start working out. I did some push-ups to start with, then a bunch of burpees. I actually felt a little better after that. I guess getting the heart pumping helped move all the damaged blood around my body. If I felt better later that day, I decided I would make another attempt at working out, too.

I guess I dozed off for a while. I woke up, got to my feet, and started pacing my cell. Back and forth I went, trying to get my body moving. Trying to fight off the chronic boredom. I was never a big reader, but I would have read the back of a cereal box right now. Anything to keep my mind stimulated. As I said earlier, it wasn't the violence that got to me; it was the crushing boredom.

Somehow, I managed to work up a good sweat from pacing back and forth. My heart rate was up (that was a good thing), and it would probably help me sleep again tonight with some exercise. Despite the light being on in the cell all day and all night, no windows, and no view through the steel outer door, I still felt my body clock was tuned to the right time. I sat down and contemplated my next moves.

Step one: get out of solitary. Step two: get hold of Sanders. Step three: get out of here and maybe move somewhere else? I had never been to Oregon or Idaho, but I had heard good things about both. Maybe I could ride up the Pacific coast once I was free and see which one I preferred. Get a new trucking job and stay on the right side of the law. No more breaking the rules. No more ratting out so-called brothers. I had a plan. My mind was made up.

To my surprise, not too much later, I heard the now-familiar clang of the slot on my cell door.

"Pass me your tray," the voice asked.

I slid it over.

A new tray was slid in. Sandwich, banana, and juice box.

"Thanks," I said.

"Five p.m.," the voice replied.

"Thanks," I repeated. And just like that, the stranger was gone. Even our pathetic little conversation felt good. So they were feeding me twice a day, not once. It was the afternoon. That was something. I decided from here on out I would eat breakfast, let the food digest, work out, walk the cell back and forth, eat dinner, let it digest, work out again, and then sleep. As pathetic as it sounded, just having some form and structure in solitary confinement really helped, helped to keep me sane in this lonely and isolated cell.

Chapter Five

I counted my visits from my waiter, or food delivery guy, or whatever you want to call him. Maybe a custodian? The guy who had earned enough trust from the guards to deliver the meals to the inmates in solitary confinement. The way I figured it, this was day six of him bringing me two meals a day. How long was solitary confinement normally in an establishment like this? A week? A month? I was new here, so maybe they did it in one week. I was hoping so. Like I keep saying, the boredom was killing me.

Your mind starts to play tricks on you after a while in solitary confinement. I remembered watching this movie, The Omega Man, as a kid, starring Charlton Heston. It was a '70s classic. In the movie, there was a war, germ warfare, or something like that. The bottom line was that he was the only man left alive, and he had free rein of the streets of Los Angeles. Only during the day, though. At night, mutants roamed the streets, and he had to lock himself up in a high-end townhouse to survive. Where was I going with all this? Oh yeah. He was so lonely that he started having auditory hallucinations that the phone was ringing. He knew no one was calling him, but he was losing it. That's how I was beginning to feel.

I did my best to keep busy: working out, meditating (well, trying to), pacing back and forth to burn off some energy. Still, it wasn't enough. I could feel myself sliding into madness.

My body was finally healing; the bruises from the beating by those two guards were beginning to fade. My ribs still hurt a lot, though.

That definitely limited me in some of the exercises I could do. But, bottom line, I was on the mend, and that was a good thing.

I woke the next morning to the sound of the slot in my steel door opening. Normally, by now I would already be awake. I guess your brain figures out, "Food will be served soon, time to wake up," or something, but this morning they woke me up.

"Slide the tray over," the voice instructed.

I did so. My old tray was taken and replaced by a new one. You guessed it: a sandwich, an apple, and a carton of milk.

"5 a.m.," the voice said. "Hang in there."

"Thanks," I replied as the slot slammed shut on me.

Sad as it was, that was the most conversation I had had since being in solitary.

Not only that, I had a peanut butter sandwich instead of turkey slices. Wow, lucky me. What a start to my day.

I ate my breakfast and sat in reflection as I waited for my food to digest. Ideally, one more day and back to the gen pop. I could do this. I wouldn't allow my mind to think I was stuck in here for another three weeks.

I was just about to start my morning burpee regimen when I heard the now-familiar clang of my steel door. Another meal? Nah. It had only been fifteen minutes. Something must have happened. Maybe Sanders had finally pulled some strings, and I was getting out of here?

To my surprise, I heard a different voice.

"Turn around and face the wall," the new voice instructed me.

A guard, or guards, I assumed. I did what I was told, bracing myself for another beating.

"Hands behind your back, Raines," the voice said. I did what I was told.

I felt pressure on the back of my neck, some form of a billy club.

"Don't try anything funny," a voice warned me.

Someone grabbed my left wrist. I felt the now-familiar steel handcuffs click tight against my wrist. Fuck, they hurt. I hated these things. Now, my right wrist.

"Back it up, asshole," said a second voice.

I walked backwards, being led by these two guards.

Had it been seven days already? Had I miscalculated? Maybe I was unconscious for the first day? I could see that being the case.

They swung me around so I was now in front of them. What was with these guys? Didn't they want me to make eye contact or something?

"Move," one of them instructed. Not quite sure where I was supposed to be going, I just kept walking. I guessed they would yank me left or right if they wanted me to turn.

We walked down a corridor filled with cells, which I assumed were much like my solitary one. You couldn't see or hear anybody, but I was convinced there were others locked up, as I had just been.

We got to another gate and waited. I guess there were security cameras above us (I couldn't see them because of the angle we were at), and moments later, the door buzzed.

"Push it open, asshole," said one of my charming escorts.

I contemplated using my head to shove it open, but went with my foot instead.

We were back in D Wing. I recognized some of the faces in the shared communal area as we entered.

"Upstairs. Move," instructed my friendly buddy.

Some of the prisoners I recognised noticed my return. They started nudging their buddies and saying stuff.

To my surprise, guys started cheering and clapping. They didn't know me, but they were obviously aware of what had happened in the food hall. Not going to lie, it actually felt good to be welcomed back.

We reached the second-floor landing. Some guys hanging out on the balcony saw me and nodded. Word spread fast around these parts, I guess.

More guys started clapping.

"Come on. Move," instructed the grouchy guard. Yeah, whatever, buddy. After being locked up for a week, it was nice to be recognized for my, ahh, "achievements."

Finally, we were on my balcony. I turned and led them to my cell. Honestly, I expected most of my stuff to have been stolen. At first glance, it certainly seemed everything was still there.

"Face the wall," my friend with the personality bypass instructed.

I faced the wall. The two guards grabbed my wrists while one of them worked the key to pop the cuffs off. I wouldn't give them the satisfaction of knowing, but it felt good to get them off my wrists.

"Just watch your step," said the other guard as they backed out of my cell and made their escape.

It felt so good to be out of that cell. I never much liked people, but after a week's deprivation, I was glad to see this motley crew of rogues and villains.

I washed my face and was about to brush my teeth when I heard a voice behind me.

"Yo, Raines. Grab your papers and come with me."

Chapter Six

"Papers? What do you mean?" I asked the stranger.

"Your prison paperwork. Come on, man. Your charges. We can't keep Milo waiting," the stranger explained.

I grabbed my charge sheet and folded it up. Who was Milo?

I turned to face the newcomer.

"You got your shit? Alright, let's go. Follow me," he instructed.

Who was this guy? And why should I be following him? Normally, I would stop and ask questions, but after a week of solitary confinement, for some reason, I decided to just go with the flow.

"Oh shit, I'm Austin, by the way," the stranger said, turning and reaching out his hand for me to shake.

"Hey, Austin. I'm John, but my friends call me Razor," I said, shaking his hand.

"Nice to meet you, bro," said Austin.

We started down the stairs to the communal part of D-Wing.

"So who's Milo?" I asked.

"Oh, Milo? He's the shot caller for this wing, bro," Austin explained. "Nothing happens on our wing without his say-so. Ya get me?"

So, basically, Milo was like the club president. Got it. I don't know why, but when someone said "shot caller," my brain defaulted to "shot putter", a big difference.

We made it down to the ground floor, and Austin led me over to a table on the far side of the room. There I spied a man in his early 50s, with an impressive beard and slicked-back hair.

"Milo. He's here," said Austin.

The two heavily tattooed men with shaved heads on either side of Milo got up and walked a short distance away, basically just out of earshot.

Milo looked up and gestured for me to come and sit down next to him.

I stepped forward.

"John Raine? Right?"

Milo had done his homework.

"Yes, nice to meet you, Milo," I said, extending my hand. He didn't take it.

"Got your papers on you?" he asked.

I handed him my charge sheet.

Milo took a moment to examine it. He handed it back to me.

"Oh shit. You were part of the Desert Phantoms crew that the Feds took down?" he asked.

"Yeah. That was us," I replied.

"Damn, you guys were high rollers," he said. "Anything you need on the car, you ask me."

"Car?" I asked.

"Yeah, D-Wing," said Milo, looking at me like I was an idiot.

"Oh, yeah. Duh. I get ya," I replied.

"Oh yeah," said Milo. "Good job with Trey. That was impressive."

"Who's Trey?" I asked.

"That's the dude who came at you in the food hall, bro," explained Milo.

"Oh. I didn't think. You get in my face like that, I just react," I replied.

"Yeah, fair enough. That's how it should be," said Milo. "Truth is, Trey is one of our guys. He was just putting in the work."

"Putting in the work?" I asked.

"Oh. Everyone has to put in the work here," Milo replied. "He was mud-checking ya."

"Mud-checking?" I started to reply.

"Yeah! He was seeing what you were made of," smiled Milo. "He found out."

"So he was one of yours?" I asked.

"Yeah. For survival and our safety's sake, we have to test any newcomers. See what they are made of. You will learn in time. You want to survive; we have to stick together. There is no room for weakness. The second someone starts on you, take 'em out. If you are perceived as weak in here, well, you won't survive."

"Makes sense," I replied.

"So, you need anything, man?" Milo asked me.

Now, to be honest with you, I had heard as a kid: you borrow something from someone in prison, well, you usually have to pay it back, whether that means money-wise (usually some overly inflated price) or through sex. No way was I having sex with any dudes. Money? All my money was gone, taken after the Feds arrested me.

Some laws say that if any of your earnings are tied to criminal activities, they can take everything from you. I had to ask him to clarify.

"Thanks, Milo. That's very kind of you, but what's the catch?" I asked.

He looked at me for a moment, almost sizing me up. He paused, as if he was choosing his words carefully.

"No catch," he replied. "Think of it as a welcoming present."

"Ahh. Okay," I replied, still not sure where this was going.

"Look, man. No need to get paranoid. We do this for all newcomers we deem worthy. It's all about survival in here. Other groups have the numbers. We have fewer numbers, so we only accept the worthy. We see you as a worthy member, bro."

"Well, ah, thanks," was all I could think of to reply to Milo.

Milo looked at one of his buddies, who was standing back. He gave a slight nod. The man walked forward with a small kit bag.

"Here you go, brother," he said, sliding it across the table to me.

"Thanks," I replied. "Much appreciated."

"Clearly, you are new to the prison system," said Milo. "Stick with us, and we will look out for ya. Show you the ropes. Teach you the rules."

"Thanks, Milo," I replied.

"Yeah, rule number one," said the shaven-headed thug standing beside Milo, "never snitch."

Chapter Seven

I started hanging out with Milo's crew all the time. They were actually a good bunch of guys making the most of a bad situation. Not everyone behind the wall is a truly evil person. Some of the guys made colossal mistakes and were paying the price. You have one beer too many but are still perfectly in control and drive home. Some dude steps out in front of your car; you accidentally hit him, but because you are technically over the limit, it's murder. Some of the guys never got to go to school, for whatever reason, and turned to crime to support themselves. Uncle Sam doesn't like people who don't pay taxes. Into prison you go.

We ate breakfast together, we worked out together, and we watched TV together. We rolled as one unit through the entire D Wing. There really was truth to the saying, "strength in numbers."

The guys encouraged me to… wait for it… Get a job. Pay in prison was a joke. Like, we are talking about forty cents an hour or something. You could use that money at the end of the month to buy snacks and whatnot from the prison commissary. Some guys had parents who put money on their books every month so they could buy candy bars and taco chips, but most had to find a way to earn money inside.

Austin was telling me it wasn't just about the money. It was about making the day go by faster by staying occupied and earning a useful skill for when you are back out in the so-called "free world." He raised some good points, but in my mind, at least at that stage in prison, I didn't see the point. Agent Sanders was coming back. Agent Sanders was going to pull some strings. I intended to be out of here in no time. No sense in taking a prison job from someone when I would be back out driving big rigs in a matter of weeks.

Speaking of Agent Sanders, any chance I had, I called his office. For two weeks, I got the runaround: "Yes, I will take a message," "Yes, Mr Raines, I passed on your message," "Yes, Mr Raines, I am sure he will call you back when he can," and on and on. I was beyond frustrated, but honestly, this was pretty much how it was dealing with any government employee, from the Tax Department to the Department of Motor Vehicles. You just had to keep trying and not give up.

One morning, when the guys were getting ready to go to work, one of the guards approached me.

"Raines. You have a visitor," he said.

I got up to be escorted to the visitors' room.

I wasn't expecting anyone. I had no family here, and the family I had back east, well, we were not on talking terms. It had to be Sanders!

Okay, scratch that. As we left D Wing and headed to the visitors' room, the guard led me to the right, into a different part of the adjoining building. So, not a regular visitor? I assumed someone high up in the prison system. Corrections captain? Associate warden, perhaps?

The guard led me down a pristine white corridor with coloured lines painted on the floor. Finally, we came to a section with doors on the right and some benches bolted to the floor out front.

"Take a seat," my guard instructed. I sat down. The guard opened one of the doors and spoke to someone out of my view.

"Hey, I have him here now. You ready for him? Oh, okay," said my guard. From where I was sitting, I could not hear what the person (or persons) inside the room was saying in reply. I guessed I would soon find out.

The guard turned back to me.

"Okay, you can go in now," he said. "You've got one hour."

Were they just going to leave me in a room with someone? What was this?

The guard watched me enter the room. I saw a suit-and-tie guy with a buzz cut. Didn't look much like a lawyer to me.

"If he acts up, just hit the panic button. I won't be far away," said the guard from behind me before shutting the door.

"I'll be fine," said Mr suit-and-tie.

"Who are you?" I asked.

"Have a seat, John," said Mr suit-and-tie.

I sat at one end of the table. From what I could tell, this was some sort of client–attorney room. I knew from talking to the guys that the visitors' room was heavily monitored. Basically, anything you said to a wife, girlfriend, or a person visiting you would be overheard in the visitors' room. Legally, they were not allowed to listen in on meetings with lawyers, under the attorney–client privilege or whatever it was called. At least I hoped that was the case.

The suit-and-tie guy sat at the other end of the table and stared at me.

"I'm Agent Beasley from the Bureau of Enforcement for Substances, Arms, and Contraband (BESAC) Phoenix office. Heard a lot about you," said Mr suit-and-tie.

"Okay…" I replied. "Where's Sanders?"

"Sanders is in Washington, D.C.," Beasley replied.

"Whoa, that's one long court case," I replied.

"Oh, that case was done two weeks ago," Beasley explained.

"What?" I asked.

"Yes, he got transferred to D.C.," explained the agent.

Ah, shit. Here it is. I am so screwed. This isn't good.

Chapter Eight

"So, is he coming back at all?" I asked.

"Not as far as I am aware," replied Agent Beasley.

Fuck.

"Um, okay, so…" I started to say.

"It is my understanding that you had a deal with Sanders," Beasley interrupted me.

"Well, I was working for him," I said, quite confident the guards were not recording our conversation.

"You were a confidential informant," stated Beasley.

"Correct," I replied.

"Before we go any further, I think I should let you know something," said Beasley.

"What's that?" I asked.

"Me, personally," said Agent Beasley, "I can't stand confidential informants. In my personal experience, they do similar crimes, or even worse, and set up other people for lengthy incarceration terms."

"Okay," I replied.

Internally, my heart sank. I knew I was totally screwed.

"However, with all that said, I do acknowledge that you and Agent Sanders had a working relationship."

"Well, we did," I replied, feeling just a glimmer of hope.

Agent Beasley opened the giant file folder he had sitting in front of him. He started flicking through the papers, trying to find something.

"Ah, here," he said finally.

"Um, okay…" I replied.

"Sanders tasked you with gathering enough evidence to arrest one 'Travis Monroe'. Is that correct?" Agent Beasley asked.

"Well, kind of. Basically, information that would lead to the arrest of any of the Desert Phantoms Motorcycle Club," I replied.

Beasley consulted his paperwork.

"Well, checking his notes here, he specifically says Travis Monroe, which you failed to do."

"Yes, but I did a lot of other things," I countered.

"Let me check that," said Beasley. "Yes, you did do a lot of other things. You ran over a cameraman, killing him. You led law enforcement on a high-speed police chase, and you were caught with a significant quantity of high-grade crystal meth."

Oh damn, this guy was a hard-ass.

"Well, actually, the other guy was driving and let me take the rap," I lied.

Agent Beasley reviewed his case files again.

"It says here three different peace officers witnessed you confessing to driving the truck. So how did this passenger get you to confess?" he asked.

"I was dazed after the truck crashed." Lame response, I know, but I couldn't think of what else to say.

"Sorry, Raines, you will have to try harder than that. I am just going by the facts, and it doesn't look good," Beasley replied.

"Well, what about all the bad guys I helped put away?" I asked.

"Well, my understanding of that is you were paid very handsomely for your assistance in those particular cases. That was your reward for helping us, Raines," said Beasley.

I was losing my patience with this guy.

"Look, man. I know you are the new guy here and you're playing catch-up on a case that's not yours, but I can't be in here."

I put all my cards on the table with this fucker.

"I'm sorry, John. You killed a man. What do you expect me to do?" Agent Beasley replied.

"Uh, get me out of here?" I asked.

"Look, I get it. You were working with Sanders, but that doesn't give you a 'get out of jail free' card. We are not playing Monopoly here, Raines. This is real life. We are not talking about making a minor shoplifting charge go away here, pal. This is serious shit."

"Well, it was an accident. It was something that happened while I was working for you guys!" I belted out. "There has to be a protocol in place for situations like this!"

Beasley sighed.

"Yes, John, we have protocols for this. If one of our own agents did something like this, guess where he would be?" asked Beasley.

"In prison?" I replied.

"Correct. That's one of our own agents, not some low-life who goes about slinging life-destroying drugs," he replied.

"So that's it?" I asked. "I'm just supposed to rot in here?"

"Well, what did the criminal underworld use to say? 'If you can't do the crime, don't do the crime.' Remember that saying, Raines?"

"Yes, I remember. In my defense, I was doing all of this for you," I replied.

"Maybe so, but as I said, if you were a federal agent and you did these things, you would be right where you are, too. What makes you think you deserve anything different?"

We were just going round and round here. I felt sick. I felt pissed off. I needed to clear my head. There had to be another way out of this. There was always another strategy. Another play to be had.

"So you can't do anything for me?" I asked.

Agent Beasley sighed again.

"I will tell you what. I will go meet with my bosses next week. I can't promise anything, but I'll see if I can get you moved to another prison, something more country club. How's that?"

That was better than rotting in this hellhole for the next twenty years.

"Okay. Thanks, man. I appreciate it," I replied.

"No promises, but I will do my best," said Beasley.

"Oh, sorry for snapping at you before. I am just very frustrated."

"Understood," said Agent Beasley. "Look, just thinking out loud here, it would probably be smart if you refer to me as your lawyer. You get me?"

"Yes. Good thinking. Thanks."

Beasley was right. If word got around that I was meeting some dude in a smart suit, the residents of this fine establishment might think I was working for the cops.

Beasley closed his file, got up, and banged on the door. Moments later, the same guard who had escorted me to this interview room stuck his head in.

"All done?" he asked.

"Yes. Thanks, Sargent Taylor. You can take him back to his cell now," Agent Beasley replied.

"Prisoner Raines. Come with me," said the guard. "Do you remember the way to the front office?"

"Yes, thanks. I can see myself out," Agent Beasley replied.

Sargent Taylor escorted me back to D-Wing.

"Is that your lawyer?" he asked.

"Yes," I replied, deep in thought.

Back in my cell, I brooded. My chances of getting out of this hellhole were not good. I had to be the master of my own destiny. I had to start thinking about planning an escape.

Chapter Nine

The next few weeks were a blur for me, waking up, eating breakfast, working out with the guys, reading books, and staying out of trouble. When the guys were at their various jobs, I stayed in my cell and read. At least out of solitary confinement, I could keep my mind busy by reading and, of course, socializing.

One day, just after lunchtime, I was lying in my cell reading The Lord of the Rings when I heard someone knocking on my cell door. I put my book to one side and looked up. It was the dude who had jumped me in the food hall a month ago. I jumped to my feet, ready to fight.

"No dude, chill, it's all good," the stranger said.

Yeah, right, I thought.

He held up his hands in a "I surrender" pose, like you would do to cops when they're pointing a gun at you.

"Okay, talk," I said.

"Well, first off, my name is Trey," he said.

"Hey, Trey. John," I replied.

"No hard feelings about last month, John," Trey said. "You got a nice right hook. I didn't see it coming."

"Um, thanks?" I replied.

"Yeah, you definitely rocked me," Trey smiled.

"Um, okay?" I said again.

"Look. Here's how it works. Part of my job, putting in the work, is that I have to mud-test new guys," Trey explained. "We have to test their mettle. See what they're made of."

"Yeah, Milo was saying something about that," I replied.

"We are a small, tight-knit bunch of guys here," Trey continued. "We are heavily outnumbered, and we gotta know anyone who rolls with us can hold their own."

"Understood," I said, slightly letting down my guard.

"You mind if I come in?" Trey asked.

"Sure," I replied, gesturing for him to step into my cell.

"Thanks, bro," said Trey. "I just got out today."

"Huh? What?" I asked. I thought he meant he had been in solitary all this time. A month? I would be a basket case after a month living like that. He seemed in good spirits.

"Yeah, when you and I fought, I got put in the hole for a month. Sucks ass," Trey smiled.

Damn, he was taking it a lot better than I would have. I guess it got easier over time.

"You were in all this time? Wow. I would have lost my damn mind," I replied.

"All good, bro. Gets easier the more you go back. Besides, it gives me a break from being on the main line, no more falling asleep listening to guys crying, snoring, farting, screaming. You know what I'm saying."

"Yeah, good points," I replied.

“That said, I swear when I get out, I’m never doing another push-up. Never again,” Trey said. “The boys have been showing you the ropes?”

“Yeah, kinda. Gave me a welcome package, shaving cream, razors, stuff like that,” I replied.

“Oh, that’s cool. We try to do that for all the guys who come in,” Trey explained.

“Did they give you a friendly?” asked Trey.

“What's a friendly?” I asked. Clearly, I was not up on prison slang.

“It’s a knife that can pass through the metal detectors,” Trey explained.

“Eh, I should be good,” I replied. I didn’t see any need for weapons. Why earn yourself another trip to solitary confinement? Screw that.

“Well, no problem. If you ever do, just ask, bro,” said Trey.

“Thanks,” I replied.

We hung out longer and shot the shit, talking about everything from what we did outside in the so-called “free world” to how long each of us had left. He had seven more years, and I, well, who knew at this stage? Worst-case scenario, I wasn’t getting out until age 70.

Turns out Trey was in the cell two down from mine. In time, we would become fast friends. Who knew the guy you ended up fighting on your first day would become one of your best bros on the inside? Weird how it all works out, eh?

Around 5 p.m., the rest of the boys returned from their daily work assignments. Despite it being great to see them, I was still not prepared to try any of the "work" on offer. The way I looked at it back then, it was slave labour. Screw that, and screw the authorities who profited off the boys' hard work.

That evening, we collectively headed to the food hall for dinner. I was starving and couldn't wait to see what they had to offer. Usually, on a Thursday night, we had meatloaf. Most of the food inside was pretty dire, but whoever was in charge of the meatloaf did a good job. I couldn't wait.

Standing a few guys ahead of us in line was the biggest, meanest-looking steroid monster you had ever seen. At least 6'4" and probably close to 300 lbs of pure muscle, he was the stuff nightmares were made of. I tell you right now, you would NOT want to fight a guy like that. Just one punch would probably put you in a coma for a month.

I turned my back to speak to Milo for a moment. Just as I was mid-sentence, Milo said,

"Oh shit!"

I turned to see a tiny little Hispanic guy, probably no more than 130 lbs soaking wet, stabbing the muscle-bound behemoth. Quick, short stabs into the man mountain's vital organs. The huge dude went down.

Alarms went off.

We were forced to hit the ground face down, arms up. Guards flooded the food hall.

I guess no meatloaf for me tonight.

It took about an hour to clear everything up. We were led back to D-Wing, and everyone was put into lockdown.

I was so pissed off. I wanted that damn meatloaf.

Finally, they announced they would bring us food to our cells.

Alright, maybe I would get my meatloaf after all.

It took till nine p.m. to finally get served, but I got my precious meatloaf, stone cold, but still well needed.

As I ate my food in my cell, I made up my mind. I would ask Trey for a "friendly" tomorrow. If a guy like that can get taken out by a little dude practically one-third of his size, then none of us were safe.

Chapter Ten

One of the things I liked best about those days was Sunday afternoons. We had our section out on the yard, and we would just shoot the shit and trade stories about life in the free world, stories about growing up, stories about our criminal escapades, stuff like that. Despite all of us growing up in different parts of America, we were all wild kids running amok in our little part of the country.

Of course, I couldn't go into much detail about what I did crimewise back in New York City. You never knew when someone might be transferred back East, or someone from the East Coast might be transferred to Coyote Ridge. If I gave too many details about our drug operation, it wouldn't take a genius to figure out who I really was and what I did to avoid going to prison. All I could do was share stories about nightclubbing and girls in 80s and 90s New York. Regardless, the guys loved it.

Austin and his pals had a great little criminal enterprise going. He and his crew would rob stores in shopping malls. They would come in during the day, scout stores, find which ones had security cameras on the outside but not inside, figure out what to steal, and come in from the roof. You see, back in those days, security camera technology wasn't great, and it was pretty pricey. Not all stores had cameras inside. Besides, many of them figured if you were in the mall, the mall's security cameras would catch you, so why invest in an in-house system?

They would scale the rooftops of shopping malls at night and find their target store. Remove the air conditioning unit and climb down into the building. One of his buddies on the roof would be waiting to hoist up their bounty by ropes, and then they would make their escape. Once back at their warehouse, they would either sell the items locally on the black market or ship them to Mexico to be sold there.

The genius and downfall of their organized thieving ring were these. They had heard about people getting busted for crimes by their shoe prints. I think that Night Stalker guy in LA got done like that. Wearing a rare shoe in a certain size, you leave a footprint at the crime scene, and they catch you. So before each run, Austin would go to a Payless shoe store and pick up some cheap, say $20 sneakers with a distinctive sole pattern. As soon as they had successfully left their shopping mall at night, they would ditch those shoes in a local dumpster. The logic being, if law enforcement ever raided their homes and checked their shoes, they would not find a match. So far, so good. Made sense to me.

They had a couple of close calls with night watchmen. One time, they were robbing a computer store of high-end laptops when a security guard inside the mall spotted them. He scrambled madly to find the right keys to unlock the store from inside the mall, then ran to a back room and made their escape through the ceiling. By the time the guard got into the store, they were in the mall car park, starting their van up to leave. When the guard had figured out how they had made their escape and run to the rear car park, all he saw were taillights.

Obviously, here in Phoenix, the roofs of buildings get hot in the summer. Okay, scratch that, they get crazy hot in the summer. Most professional buildings have that black tar on their roofs. So the guys would leave shoe prints. They had already covered that problem by buying those off-brand, cheapo sneakers from Payless.

Somewhere along the way, they must have made a print or two of these unique sneakers. That was fine; none of the guys kept a pair of these sneaks in their closets, so they couldn't be tied to the robberies. So far, so good, right? Wrong.

They must have suspected Austin, or kept a close eye on him. For when they finally dragged him in for "questioning," he denied owning a sneaker like that, with that sole pattern. The cops were two steps ahead of him. They produced pictures of him in two separate Payless shoe stores purchasing set after set of these sneakers. One of his guys rolled over for a reduced sentence, and Austin and his crew got lengthy prison terms. Hearing stuff like that made me see how much people hated snitches.

Trey's story was the same, but different. He and his crew would rob corporate motorcycle chains all over the Southwest of our great nation. They would hit Nevada, California, Utah, Colorado, and even Idaho once.

They would scope out a big showroom, figure out what to steal, come back at night, disable the alarm systems, ram-raid the showroom doors, get in, grab everything of value, and be gone in two minutes. Once back in Arizona, they would strip some bikes for parts, sell some to Mexico, and sell others via classified ads in local newspapers.

The one time they travelled as far as Idaho to steal bikes, they nearly got caught. I guess when you have a large box truck that *could* be holding a ton of stolen bikes, Highway Patrol is going to want to pull you over to check what you are carrying. One of their guys was following behind them and had to create a distraction, abusing the state troopers, so they had to give up their roadside pull-over and go chase the car. Close call. After that, they decided to stick to the states closer to Arizona for their thievery.

Trey had a nice circle of independent motorcycle shops in Arizona he could sell parts to, and sometimes even a full bike if it was what his buyer was looking for. Pretty sure the guys knew everything was "hot," but for the prices Trey was selling at, it was worth it for them not to ask any serious questions. Life was good.

But as always, when life is good from you doing illegal things, life has a way of coming back around and biting you in the ass. That's exactly what happened to Trey and his crew.

After a particularly successful haul from a Harley dealership in Southern California, Trey and his guys had more scoots than they knew what to do with. One of his guys, I forget his name, but he was living up in Flagstaff, apparently, thought it was a good idea to sell them online. Flagstaff's a college town, and he figured he could easily move Sportsters to students. This time, he was stuck with a couple of Fat Boys he couldn't sell to college kids, so he had the bright idea of posting on a MySpace forum (MySpace being the precursor to Facebook, kids).

As progressive as that thinking was, one of the detectives up in Flagstaff was also forward-thinking enough to be monitoring online forums for stolen bikes. Law enforcement played it smart. They sent over a geeky-looking detective; he asked all the right questions and then bought the bike. A short time later, Trey's brother did the same thing, put another bike up on the same MySpace forum, and the cops sent another guy over as a quiet family man looking to purchase a high-end Harley for a very reasonable price. Yeah, you guessed it, they had him now.

After the second stolen bike sale to an undercover cop, it was only a matter of time. Once they started purchasing bikes from other states and not just California, it became clear that Trey's crew was the one they were looking for. Because they were transporting them over state lines, it became a federal crime.

Trey's guy rolled over and gave up everyone. Knowing they had him dead to rights and not having enough money for a high-powered legal team, Trey accepted a plea deal. I tell you, the Feds only ever wanted to take sure-fire winning cases; that's why their success rate was so high. If it wasn't a slam-dunk case, they weren't interested.

Trey ended up getting 20 years, eligible for parole in 15. All in all, he was in good spirits about the whole thing, but was keen to get back out and ride again. That I could understand. I had to admit I missed the open road, too.

Chapter Eleven

Out on the street, I was never one for politics. Democrat? Republican? All the same to me. It was like going to the casino and declaring, "I'm for red," or "I'm for black." Didn't matter which one you put your money on, sooner or later, the house would take it all. Someone once said to me, "No matter who you vote for, the government wins." That was always my attitude growing up.

Here, in prison, there was a different form of politics. You could not ignore it either. Ignoring it would mean your death. There were different cliques, divided by race. There were groups divided by prison wings. None of that really mattered. What did matter was this: someone calls you a punk or a rat, you had to fight. Not fighting would be the end of you. Can't take it? Want to roll it up, check out, and go into protective custody? Well, guess what? They can still get at you on PC. Not only that, no matter where you went in this prison, or any other, you would forever be labelled a sissy or a punk. The rest of your incarceration would be sour. You were then tarnished. Probably better off killing yourself than rolling it up and going into protective custody.

I was walking to the prison library one day. I had to walk through the B Wing building to get there. For some reason, all the cells on the ground floor were in lockdown, whereas the next two levels were open. Weird, but okay. I figured B Wing, different building. They probably had their own way of doing things. Some of the guys had little hand mirrors out so they could see who was coming and going through their block.

One of the guys in the middle of the block saw me and started calling out. I couldn't hear what he was saying, so I got closer to him. Then I realized he was calling me a "rat." He was part of the Black Scorpions gang, which was affiliated with one of the bigger cartels (I forget which), probably serving as foot soldiers for the cartel, doing their dirty work on the streets of Arizona.

Apparently, I looked like someone he knew, or thought he knew, but whatever the story was, he had me mixed up. Sure, I was a rat, well, a paid informant, but not on him or his crew. Prison politics dictated I shut him up there and then, or else. I couldn't get to him as he was locked in his cell, so I did the next best thing. I spat on him. That was it. B Wing went silent. Everyone waited to see what would happen next.

He started hollering in Spanish, and one of his buddies from the second tier ran down. He grabbed me and started shouting. I told him I didn't speak any Spanish and to tell his buddy that I was no rat.

The two guys had a heated exchange. I was then informed by the younger guy that we had to fight. Since they were currently locked up, it wasn't happening today, but I would have to fight him out on the yard tomorrow. I was backed into a corner. I had to fight or be marked as a sissy. I had been in enough fights that I wasn't overly concerned about fighting this guy one-on-one, but who was to say that his crew wouldn't jump in and rat-pack me?

Not only that, but this was Coyote Ridge Penitentiary. There were guards along the wall in their watchtowers with rifles. They had no qualms about shooting you. I was more concerned with getting shot than fighting some gang member. I told him I would be there, then made my excuses and left.

I went to the library, browsed for a few minutes, and gave up. Not in the mood anymore. My mind was more focused on tomorrow's fight. This was prison life. One minute, it was boring and tedious; the next minute, you're fighting some guy because he thinks you ratted his bros out. When I walked back through B Wing, I felt every eye on me. Fuck them. I would fight their guy. Win or lose, I had to show heart. That was all I could do to save face.

I made it back to D Wing unscathed. When the boys returned from their jobs, I told them what had transpired. Milo and Austin said they would get out of their work detail to watch my back in the yard. That was somewhat reassuring, but at the same time, I felt that part of them just wanted to watch a fight to get some action going in their lives.

I slept poorly that night, going over all the ways the fight could possibly play out the next day. As I said, my biggest concern wasn't getting my ass kicked one-on-one, but getting rat-packed by his crew or getting shot by the tower guards. In the end, I fell asleep trusting that whatever higher power there was above me would take care of me. Lame, but that was all I had.

The morning passed in a blur. I couldn't think of anything else but this fight. In hindsight, if the fight had just happened spontaneously, it would have been no big deal. The anticipation was worse than anything else.

By lunchtime, it seemed that everyone in the food hall knew what was going to go down that afternoon. I would guess some guys had money on the fight. Actually, scratch that, I guarantee you some guys had money on the fight.

Finally, it was yard time. Milo and Austin led me to the one patch of the yard where there was a blind spot from our tower buddies. My buddy from B Wing turned up with about eight in his crew. If they did decide to rat-pack me, then Austin and Milo would have their hands full trying to fight them off. Both groups created a circle around us, and we squared off.

My accuser was bigger than he had appeared in his cell, but I had fought guys bigger than him before. Sometimes big guys weren't great fighters, but all it took was one lucky punch, and you were going to be picking your teeth off the floor. Really, thinking about it, anyone could beat anyone in a fight on any given day, especially if you were not in a ring and there was no referee. I wouldn't be surprised if Buddy Boy's pals were all carrying shanks. Actually, thinking about it, I was sure Austin and Milo were armed too.

We circled each other, mutually sizing up our opponent. I shot a few jabs, more to gauge the distance between us and test his reaction time. He was fast, but maybe not fast enough. He tried a few on me, and I could tell he had some fight training. I would have to stay out of the way of his right hand, that was for sure.

I faked a left and swung a right. Not my best shot, but it connected with his temple and definitely rocked him. He rhino-charged me, grabbing my shirt and hitting me multiple times in the guts. Thankfully, all the workout sessions with the boys had turned my once-flabby beer belly into tight abs. Yes, it knocked the wind out of me a bit, but not enough to take me out of the fight.

I managed to get my arm around his neck like a reverse headlock. Using my left leg, I tripped him up, sending us both to the dirt. I landed on top of him, knocking the wind out of him. I managed to move my body around enough to get some blows to his face. Hitting someone in the face can be very misleading. Usually, it results in a lot of blood, but it rarely takes the fight out of an opponent. I guess the best way to describe it was: it looks worse than it actually is. Apparently, I messed him up enough, though, as his buddies started pulling me off him. To their credit, none of them tried to rat-pack me. With adrenaline pumping through me, it took me a moment to calm down.

His pals lifted him to his feet and, to my surprise, he stuck out his hand to shake. For some reason, I took it and shook it. He then admitted he was mistaken about me being a rat and apologized. That had to be a first. He told me his name was Santos and that I was a-okay in his book. Alright then…

Chapter Twelve

Word spread throughout the prison's wings about the fight. The only people who love gossip more than little old ladies are hardened prisoners. I tell ya. Now you would think winning a fight against someone from a feared prison gang would be a good thing, right? Like, "Stay away from that guy, he beat up Santos from the Black Scorpions," that kind of thing. Nope. It kinda made it worse in a way. Because now you had a name for yourself as a fighter. So what does everyone want to do? They want to beat you so they can brag about it. Screw that. I fought Santos to be left alone, not to attract more fights. I got lucky one time. I mean, we could have easily been shot by the guards. How many more times was I prepared to test my luck?

I had to get out of here. I needed to escape. If the Feds were not going to help me or did not want to help me, then I needed to take matters into my own hands.

I thought about it. I tried to think back to every prison escape movie I had seen before and run through the options. What did I know? What would be most feasible?

Land a helicopter in the yard? Insanity. It would never work. The pilot would be shot dead before he even had a chance to land.

Have someone fire a rocket launcher through one of the prison walls? Blast a hole big enough, then run through it to a waiting getaway car? Sure, in the chaos, you might have stunned some of the watchtower guards, but it's still totally unrealistic, like something out of a Hollywood movie. Maybe you take out one of the watchtower guards, but the rest would open fire on you (and your pals on the outside) before you even had a chance to run to safety. Forget it. Terrible idea.

What else? Hmm... overpower some guards? Steal their uniforms and try to trick your way out? Nah, no chance.

Riot? Take over the prison and negotiate a way out? Nah, no chance of that ever happening. Those hostage negotiator guys are tricky bastards. They would stall just long enough to send in the SWAT team to take back the prison. Forget it.

I had heard stories about guys swapping clothes with someone on the outside and walking out like a visitor. Ballsy move, but I doubt that would work in a prison like this. Maybe some low-security country-club-style prison, but definitely not in an old-school joint like this. No chance. No way.

Right around the time I was running through ideas to break out of prison, my next-door cell neighbor killed himself, or as we used to call it inside, “he took early parole.” Yeah, morbid humor, but that was kind of how we had to handle it inside. Apparently, a lot of new guys freak out and would rather kill themselves than face their sentence. Fair enough. I could see a guy with no hope choosing to take his own life rather than face 20 years of this shit. Without hope, we had nothing.

Trey took the opportunity to move into the now-empty cell. Before this, he was two cells away; now he was my next-door neighbor. I asked him if it bothered him that someone had died in the cell he was taking over, and he told me it didn’t. He said something like, “If you really think about it, there was probably someone who had died in every cell in this place," so you just had to push it out of your mind. Fair enough, I guess.

Where was I? Oh yeah, running through the options for escaping Coyote Ridge. I remembered reading about a guy who did yoga for months, managed to fold himself into a tiny spot in a laundry hamper, and got out that way. Not a bad idea, but could I honestly see myself doing yoga for six months just to try and tie myself up into a pretzel? Not doable. Maybe for some guys, but not me.

I was almost out of ideas, and then it hit me. *Escape from Alcatraz!* I saw that movie at the theater as a kid and loved it. Clint Eastwood was a big action hero right before Arnie and Sly came along. He and three pals are stuck on the infamous Alcatraz prison island and dig their way out. The prison building is so old and crumbly that it might just work here, too.

Now that Trey was my neighbor, maybe it was something I could get him on board with, too.

Chapter Thirteen

Trey wasn't in the yard that afternoon. I saw him at the chow hall the following morning and asked when he would next be on the yard. Sure, we could have talked at dinner, but you could never tell who was listening in to your private conversations at mealtime. The yard made more sense, where there were plenty of places to talk out of earshot of fellow crims.

"Hey, Trey, when are you out on the yard next?" I asked.

Trey thought for a moment.

"Tomorrow afternoon," he replied. "Why? What's up?"

"Gotta talk to ya," I replied.

"Oh shit," Trey whistled. "Everything okay?"

"Yeah, man, no complaints," I said. "Just got something to run by you. That's all."

Trey looked around the chow hall.

"Yeah. I got you," he said. "Say no more. We can speak tomorrow. Okay?"

"Yeah, thanks, brother," I replied.

When we sat down to eat, neither Trey nor I let on to Austin and Milo that we planned to speak the next day in the yard. We were in cool lockstep.

The next day dragged. I could see why most of the guys pushed to get work assignments inside. I mean, the money was a joke, like, pitiful. Not sure what the minimum wage was back then, but let's say, for argument's sake, it was five dollars an hour. Inside, we were getting like thirty to forty cents an hour. A cynic might say the only way for America, with all our unions and "workers' rights," to compete against China in keeping production costs down was prison labour.

Lock guys up on bullsh*t charges, have them so bored they're begging you to work a forty-hour week for twelve bucks? Was that right? Twelve bucks for a week's work? Math was never my strong point, but that kind of added up. I checked it twice. If it's wrong, whatever, you get the point I'm trying to make. We priced ourselves out of the job market to live the American dream; countries like China undercut us, and now the only way we could compete was by using prisoners.

I was determined not to get a prison job. I was completely focused on a plan to get out of here. That was my prime directive. Not a damn day job.

Finally, I saw everyone returning from work. We had an hour until chow. This was my time. I had run through scenarios in my head for pitching it to Trey. In the end, I decided the straight-out, put-it-to-him move was the best strategy.

Trey walked past my cell to his and dumped his work gear. I could hear him running the sink in his cell, washing his face, his hands. That's another thing about prison: no one has any privacy. You can hear your neighbours farting, pooping, crying, praying, whatever. Hard to have any secrets behind the wire.

Moments later, he was in front of my cell door.

"You ready for yard, bro?" Trey asked me.

"Yeah, man," I replied, dumping my book on my bed and jumping up. "Let's go."

We worked our way down the stairs amidst the chaos of the afternoon. It almost reminded me of being back in junior high, except no females to drool over. Plus, instead of teachers, we had guards with guns and bad attitudes. Yeah, slight difference, eh?

We made our way through the throng of fellow prisoners and got out into the afternoon sun. It wasn't the open road, but something definitely felt better just being outside. If you could ignore the massive twenty-foot-high stone walls, then yeah, just like the open road.

Satisfied we had sufficient distance between us and any other guys on the yard, Trey turned to me and asked:

"So what's up, man?"

I looked around again to make sure no one was in earshot. Despite being surrounded by self-proclaimed "tough guys" and real tough guys, you could never be too sure who would use your private conversations to barter for themselves a reduced sentence. I know, I know, I was once guilty of similar behaviour. Lesson learned, okay? Let it go already.

"Hey, I got an idea," I started.

"Oh boy," said Trey. It was almost like he knew it was coming.

Instinctively, I checked around again. Coast still clear.

"I wanna get out of here," I said.

"Hey man, you and me both," said Trey.

"Yeah. But I'm talking escape," I said. There, I said it.

"Whoa," Trey whistled. "Damn, you okay, bro?"

"Yeah, I'm good," I replied. "Look, if this were wartime and we were in a German prisoner-of-war camp, it would be our patriotic duty to escape."

Trey thought for a moment. "Yeah, true. But one problem, we're not at war, and this isn't Germany."

"Yeah, okay, I take your point," I replied. "But by that same logic, the general population outside of here wouldn't be as hostile to us as the German population would've been to American G.I.s trying to escape."

"Fair point, John, but let's face it, POW camps were probably easier to break out of than this rock," Trey countered.

"Well, whatever the case, guys still managed it," I argued.

"Okay, point taken," said Trey. "So what do we do once we're out?"

"Mexico," I replied. "No extradition. Cheap cost of living. We're close enough to the border."

"Sounds good," Trey said. "But how do we get out?"

"I've got some ideas," I replied. "How would you do it?"

Trey thought for a moment. "There was that case two years back in Texas."

"What case was that?" I asked.

"The Texas Seven," said Trey. "They overpowered guards, stole their guns and uniforms, and got the hell out of there."

I think I vaguely heard of that case. It rang a bell, but the details were hazy. (I'm pretty sure they all got captured, or killed, though.)

"We'd need a trustworthy crew to try something like that," I replied.

Trey considered it.

"Yeah, good point. I think we could probably count on two, maybe three solid guys," he said.

"Yeah, not enough. My thinking is the more guys we recruit, the more chance someone will snitch on us," I said.

Trey sighed. "Yeah, I get ya. It's like that old saying, 'three can keep a secret if two are dead,' or however it goes."

"Yes! Exactly!" I replied. "I'm thinking we keep it small, you, me, and maybe Milo?"

"Hmm, yeah," said Trey. "But those numbers aren't enough to overpower the guards, bro."

"Dude, I think rushing the guards is not the way to go. Too many variables. Too easy for something to go wrong. Too easy to get shot," I explained.

"Yeah, I guess," Trey replied. "So how do we do it then?"

"You ever seen the movie *Escape from Alcatraz*?" I asked.

"Yeah, man, but years ago," said Trey. "Remind me how it goes."

"Clint Eastwood and a bunch of guys dig their way out of prison," I said.

"Yeah, but weren't they on an island?" asked Trey.

"Yeah, but that makes their escape harder than ours," I replied.

"Hmm, yeah, true," said Trey.

"The way I see it, this prison is like a hundred years old, right? It seems pretty old and crumbly in places. Got to be a way to dig our way out."

"Yeah," said Trey.

"Get into some vents, or maybe the sewer system," I said.

Trey thought for a moment. "I could ask my dad to go to the library and see if he could source some architectural plans or something?"

"Great idea," I replied. "There has to be a weak link here somewhere."

"I'll get my dad to visit next week and have him do some research for us," said Trey.

"Okay, cool," I replied. "Let's see what he comes up with, and we can take it from there."

"Sounds good, bro," said Trey.

"Maybe we hold off telling Milo until we hear what your dad has to say?"

"Yeah, that makes sense. No reason to get him excited if it all comes to nothing," said Trey.

Chapter Fourteen

A couple of weeks had passed since we first started brainstorming a plan to bust out of this hell hole. As promised, Trey got word to his dad, who started looking into the structural plans for Coyote Ridge Penitentiary. Somehow he had found a copy of the plans at the State Library. Obviously he couldn't bring those in during visiting hours. The surviving plans, a copy of them, were for one wing of the prison, not each wing. However, we had to assume that each wing was identical in construction.

When Trey returned from his father's visit, he was eager to share the news with me. As it happened, there was a small service tunnel running behind the rear wall of each of our cells. Since Trey's father was no architect, it was a layman's interpretation of the old set of plans, but he figured it was wide enough for someone to shimmy through. Drive a truck down there? No chance. But for electrical and plumbing access, sure, that made sense. From what his dad told him, it seemed at the far end of the building some pipes ran down to the sewage system. It would be rough going, but hey, it beats sitting in here for the next twenty years. An evening of filth to avoid twenty years of slow filth? Worth it.

So now it was down to practicalities. How do we get through to the service tunnel? We would need cutting tools, something to hack at the old bricks. A way to cover our nightly handiwork. What about the noise? Then we had to figure out a way to leave the building and clear the prison yard. Would we have to go out in the open?

Was there direct access to the sewers from our building? Trey's dad thought there was. But again, without getting in there and seeing for ourselves, we couldn't be 100% sure.

Someone once told me that 90% of entrepreneurship was problem-solving. Everything I just mentioned was a giant list of problems. We would have to solve them, break it all down into bite-sized pieces and tackle it one step at a time.

I figured a couple of screwdrivers from the machine shop could chip away at the aging bricks at the back of our cells. Was there rebar in the concrete? Did they use rebar back then? I wasn't sure, but if there was, we would need hacksaw blades or something to cut through that too. Once in prison, you find there is always someone who can get you whatever you need, for a price. How they got it? No idea, and it was wise not to ask. That person for us was Milo. He had a network of allies throughout the entire prison system. Trey was confident he could get us whatever we needed (for a price).

Getting rid of all the rock and stone debris? I remembered watching some World War Two movie as a kid where they would fill their pockets with dirt every time they got outside and discreetly dump it in the yard. That could work. But what about covering our damaged walls? The prison had an art class. We could both enroll and set up oil paintings in our cells to "practice," of course. Mix up some oil paint to match the wall colour.

What about the noise of us hacking and chopping away at the prison walls? Well, it was noisy at night in our wing, but perhaps a radio as a gift to one of Trey's neighbors might help with any extra noise coming from our respective cells.

We got started right away. Trey gave Milo a shopping list of what we needed to begin. Milo gave him a price, and Trey's dad put some money on Milo's books to be spent at the prison commissary. If I hadn't recruited Trey, I would've been screwed, as every penny I had in the bank had been taken from me by the Feds. Just like in the so-called free world, money moved everything inside the pen too.

Within two days, Milo had gotten us two screwdrivers. Needless to say without saying it, he had an idea of what we were up to. He was a solid dude, with old-school gangster morals, and there was no risk of him diming us out to the guards. These were cheap screwdrivers, the kind you could probably pick up at a dollar store for a buck. Let's face it, they were no Snap-On tools. Well, it wasn't like we were going to be wrenching on BMWs or Mercedes, was it? They just needed to not snap as we worked. No idea how Milo got them into the prison. Actually, thinking about it, I didn't want to know. The fact was, he got what we asked for, and that's all we needed to know.

The first night I attempted to work on our break-out, I waited until after lights out. Sure, it was "noisy" if you were lying in your bunk trying to drift off to sleep. But trying to pick at an aging brick and chip away at it? Forget it. I felt like everyone in the entire cell block knew what I was doing. After discussing it with Trey the next day, we figured out a better strategy. Lights out was 9:30 p.m. There was so much noise on the wing after chow that it made more sense to "go to bed" an hour earlier and be finished and done before the 9:30 p.m. headcount.

This time, it was much easier to cause damage to the back wall of our respective cells. I started making headway at the bottom right corner of my vent. Sure enough, as predicted, with the hard point of the screwdriver hacking away, the rock started crumbling quite easily.

I made sure I was done "working on my wall" by 9:25 p.m., cleaned up, and jumped into bed before the guard came by. In the morning I would have to get all the rocks and debris and dump them either on the way to the food hall or out on the yard. Both Trey and I were scheduled to start art classes that afternoon. Basically, the clock was ticking before the next cell search, which was supposed to be random, but you could usually expect one every two weeks. I needed to block the obvious hole in my wall with a blend of wadded-up wet paper and oil paint. It would never pass a real physical inspection, but a cursory glance from the guards shouldn't give the game away.

I was one of those guys who got along with 95% of the world. But there was always some asshole who didn't like me, and I sure as hell didn't like him. We had a new guy who moved into the second tier, Tito. He was one of that rare 5% who just took a disliking to me from the very get-go.

Not long after we started digging our way out of hell, Tito was transferred to our wing. The first morning after his arrival, Trey and I were headed down to breakfast, minding our own business, walking down the stairs to the ground floor. This fucker comes up right behind me and tries to trip me over. Who does that?

Chapter Fifteen

When we got to the ground floor, I turned and hissed at him. He just smiled with that stupid look on his face. Milo realized what was going on and stepped in front of him.

"Not this guy, amigo," said Milo.

Tito kept smiling and just walked away. From that moment on I knew I was going to have trouble with the guy. He might not have had anything to lose, but I had a plan. I couldn't afford to blow it now. We were making progress.

Of course, to my satisfaction, Tito tried it on in the chow line and got dragged off by the guards, no doubt to get beaten and sent to the hole for a week. Good riddance. Stupid bastard. I would happily knock his block off on the street, but I couldn't afford to get into it with him now. Not when things were finally moving forward.

That evening, after work, Trey and I started art classes. Of course, we never bothered taking it seriously, we just wanted to get our hands on oil paints and attempt to match the colour of our cells with the paints provided to us. After a lot of messing about back in my cell, I finally got something close to the colour of my wall. The good thing was the location of where we were both working, under our bunks, so if a guard shone a flashlight in the area, it kind of passed as normal. But if the patch-up job was out in the open, in daylight, it would be obvious the colours didn't match. Now that we had our paints and a way to mask our progress, we were in business. I've got to admit, it felt great to have some hope in this damn hellhole. We had no way of knowing if we could even get out of the entire prison complex, but we had to try. Without hope, I had nothing.

Trey had found that if we focused our screwdrivers on the stone next to our air vents, we could pull the vent free and use it as a makeshift door into the service tunnel area. That would definitely cut down our tunnelling time. Within the first week I had removed enough material that the entire right side of my vent had come loose. We fell into a nightly rhythm: got to "bed" at 8:30 p.m., pulled the cell door shut, worked for 50 minutes, cleared the mess up, then jumped into bed and stayed visible for the 9:30 p.m. check. After lights out, we got up again and patched the hole around our vents, then painted the plaster to match the wall. Slow going, but better to take our time and do it right than rush and get caught.

We were making good headway. Even Trey's personality had changed at the thought of us getting out of Coyote Ridge. He was far more optimistic now. One morning we were in the chow line, eager for breakfast, when out of nowhere someone sucker-punched me. One minute I was standing there, eyeing the food, and the next I was on my back, seeing stars. It took me a moment to register what had happened when I noticed a size 10 sneaker coming straight for my face. I rolled out of the way just as the foot came down where my head had been moments before. What the hell? My brain registered screaming and shouting, and then I was getting dragged across the food hall by two prison guards.

In my confusion I looked over to see both Austin and Tito being dragged away as well. It took me a moment to figure out what had just happened. Tito had just got out of solitary and sucker-punched me. In the melee, Austin had jumped in to defend me and got busted, too. What bullshit. I had done nothing wrong and I was getting taken back to the hole. Prison politics dictated I couldn't snitch on Tito. All I could say, if asked, was: *"I dunno, Warden, I must have slipped."*

No breakfast and back to solitary. That fucking Tito. I had no idea what his problem was, but this was bad. Really bad. By rights I should have beaten him senseless the first time he messed with me, but I had too much to lose. Now, with me locked up for a week, not only was I behind on my timeline to escape, but I also ran the risk of the guards tossing my cell and finding our escape route. This was the worst.

Sure enough, I was unceremoniously tossed into a solitary cell and the door slammed shut in my face. Not this again. At least they didn't beat me this time. Thank goodness for small mercies. I was so mad at that prick. If they put us in a room together right now, I would have killed him. Thunderdome style, two men enter, one man leaves. I vowed then and there he would pay for this. I wasn't sure how or when, but I would get my revenge. He would regret the day he set eyes on me. Of that I was sure.

No food, back in isolation, and losing time on breaking out of prison. What a mess. I was so angry it took me a while to clear my head. Once I calmed down, I figured I might as well work out. I've always found that strengthening the body affects the mind, make the body strong and the mind follows. It was kind of better on an empty stomach too. After doing so many burpees, push-ups, and sit-ups that I lost count, I took a break. How long was I going to be held this time? A week? Two weeks? I didn't know. I barely made it out with my sanity last time.

I guess I drifted off to sleep for a while. When I woke up, I heard the all-too-familiar clang of the gate on my cell door. Food time. By my calculations, it had to be 5 p.m. Already? Crazy. It was all too easy to lose your mind in this place. I was actually hungry. I gobbled my food down. As a rule, prison food was lousy, but I tell you, this was the best-tasting meal I had ever had in my entire life. I could have eaten two trays.

I let my food digest and, once I felt an hour or so had passed, I decided to work out again. If it helped my mental state the first time, a second workout couldn't hurt, right?

Second workout done, I was at a loss. If I had a book, that would've helped. I was so bored and lonely, I even considered counting the bricks in my cell. Desperate, eh?

At a guess, I must have fallen asleep somewhere between eleven p.m. and midnight. I was woken the next day by that familiar clang of the cell door. To my surprise, instead of just opening the hatch, they opened the full door. Was I about to get beaten down again? Insubordination? Disrespecting the guards? I braced myself for the coming pain.

"Face the wall, Raines," one of my buddies instructed.

I did what I was told, tense, waiting for that inevitable billy club across the back of my neck. Only it never came. Instead, they pulled my hands behind my back and cuffed me. I was being moved, but where to?

Chapter Sixteen

"Where ya taking me?" I asked.

"Back to your cell," stated one of the guards.

Back to my cell? This made no sense. Weird, but I wasn't going to complain. I was out of solitary, the place I hated the most in this concrete hellhole.

"Okay," was all I could say as they forced me to walk in front of them with my hands behind my back.

"One of our boys saw the whole thing. He explained you were sucker punched. So we are taking you back," said the second guard.

Sometimes the "no snitching" rule pays off. Well, at least in this one case it did.

Within minutes, I was back on my wing. Some of the regulars who hung out downstairs saw me and nodded. That was the closest I would get to a "welcome back" in this joint. Honestly, that was enough for me.

They uncuffed me in my cell and left me alone. I had missed breakfast (again), and Trey and the boys were already on work duty. I had a packet of Doritos in my cell that I had previously purchased from the commissary, so I ate them. Hardly the breakfast of champions, but whatever, I was starving and that's all I had on me.

After I ate, I checked to make sure the coast was clear and stuck my head under my bunk as if I had dropped something. I wanted to make sure that no one had discovered my work on the back wall of my cell. Nope. Untouched. All was good. I had lost one day. I would resume digging my way out this very evening. By now, I would have hoped that Trey was one night ahead of me.

I took a shower and actually managed to take a nap back in my cell before Milo and Trey got back from their work duty. Both of them were as surprised as I was to see me out of solitary confinement. Poor old Austin, it would appear he was getting a full week on his own for defending me. I owed him big time for that.

It was good to get a full meal again. Over food, Trey told me he pretty much had his vent loosened all the way around now. I reassured him that I would do my best tonight to make up for the time I had spent sitting in solitary confinement.

I asked Milo why he wasn't interested in joining us. He explained that, being on the ground floor, it was next to impossible to get any privacy or work on his vent. Although it was an unwritten rule in prison that you never look into another man's cell, being right next to the common area made it unavoidable. Hanging a sheet over his bars was seen as if you were having sex with someone, something he refused to do, even for escape purposes. The poor guy had resigned himself to serving his time.

After the yard, I decided to "turn in early" and get working on my vent. I pulled away the papier-mâché fake wall and got busy. By the time it got to head count, I had made serious progress. If I pulled hard enough with my right hand, the vent was loose in its foundation. We were actually doing this.

The next day, out on the yard, I talked to Trey. His entire vent was now free. He had yet to enter the service tunnel, as he wanted to wait for me to catch up before venturing out. We decided at this stage that the best thing we could do, once I had access to it, would be to wait until after lights out and then get into the tunnel. A lot of guys had small reading lights so they could read books after lights out, but we figured it would be best not to use one for our first attempt in case the light spilled into other dudes' cells.

By the end of the week, I had made it through the concrete, holding my vent in place. I cannot describe to you the feeling of utter success I felt at that moment. It was like I had just won the lottery. Totally illogical, of course. As far as I was concerned, we still had a million miles to go before we were free and clear. But it was something. It was the first milestone. It told me we could do this. We could actually make this work.

We decided to take our first foray into the service tunnels on Saturday night, after lights out. Most of the guys on our wing would be drunk on pruno, jailhouse wine, also known as toilet hooch. Every wing had a guy who specialized in getting all the fruit served at meals, then adding a special blend of sugar and water and fermenting it into a crude form of booze.

It was a Saturday night tradition here at Coyote Ridge. I didn't partake; in fact, before I had even been locked up, alcohol was losing its appeal for me. I enjoyed the odd beer or two on our runs, but had cut down drastically from my New York days, or even from when I first moved to Arizona. Not sure whether it was my body rejecting it as I got older or just having more important things to do, but I was never tempted to try it. Besides, I had heard stories of guys going blind drinking that crap. No thanks.

Saturday went by in a blur. Hours seemed like minutes. There was a lot of noise and jolliness from the guys on the floor that night. I am pretty sure the guards were aware that the men were drunk. I am sure their logic was that they would get loud, let off a bit of steam, and then be more complacent in the morning. If any of the prisoners turned aggressive on booze, then it would be a whole other story.

Both Trey and I took it easy that evening, turning down any offers of the illegal hooch. For the first time, head count and lights out couldn't come fast enough. We said our goodbyes to the fellas right before head count and tried to act as calm and nonchalant as we could. Meanwhile, inside, I was bursting with excitement.

We decided to give it a good hour after lights out so everyone could settle down and fall asleep. I could already hear guys down the hall on our tier snoring. It was the sound of drunk snoring, which always sounds different from sober snoring if that makes any sense. Our guard walked down the landing one last time. Technically, they were meant to check on us once an hour overnight, but from experience, we knew it was more like every three or four hours. This guy would usually take a sneaky nap or watch some TV in an office somewhere, then come back later to check on us. Just to be safe, once it was go time, we stuffed our beds with clothes in the shape of a person sleeping. It would not pass a close check, but if a guard was just walking by, it might, just might, fool them.

In the cell next to mine, I heard Trey cough three times in short succession. That was our pre-arranged cue to get started. I paused for a moment and listened carefully. I heard no telltale signs that anyone was awake or that a guard was near. It was now do-or-die time. I pulled my vent out of the wall ever so slowly and carefully. The last thing I needed was a prison snitch figuring out what we were doing. I laid the vent next to the wall so that, ideally, the moment I was in the service tunnel, I could reach back into my cell and pull it somewhat shut.

I read somewhere as a kid that if you could get your full head and one shoulder into a space, then, in theory, you should be able to get into that hole. I am not going to lie, for a moment I thought I wasn't going to make it, and they would find me at 5 a.m. jammed into the hole in the wall, half in and half out. The shame would probably be worse than the beating I would get from the guards. It was uncomfortable getting myself into the service tunnel. I am not a particularly claustrophobic sort of guy, but I was feeling it, a terrible sensation. I nearly had a panic attack, something I had never had before, but imagined would be quite horrible.

Finally, I managed to squeeze myself through. The service tunnel immediately behind our cells was not wide. We had to turn sideways to maneuver away from our cells. I did, however, make sure to reach in and at least pull my vent shut before attempting to shimmy away.

Trey was already waiting for me before he made his move. We had decided to move towards the far side of the building, away from where the guards were situated. Together we made our way down, being careful to make as little noise as humanly possible as we passed our supposedly sleeping cellmates.

Once we got to the far side of the building, we lucked out. The service tunnel was much wider there, so we didn't have to move sideways to get around. We found a way to clamber down from the third floor to the ground using bits of pipe and support beams as hand and footholds. It was a surreal moment to be on the ground floor inside the guts of our building.

Where to next, though? Left or right? We knew moving left would take us toward the food hall and possibly guards, so through sloppy sign language, we both agreed to turn right and investigate. There had to be a sewage pipe or air vent that would lead us to freedom.

We made it to the far side of the back of the building and found a manhole that would lead us down and ideally out of this place. Trouble was, we had no way of getting the cover off. We would have to brainstorm some kind of lever to lift that thing off. Despite numerous TV shows and cartoons of characters coming up through sewer pipes wearing a manhole cover like some makeshift hat, those things were heavy. We would have to come up with a solution for our second hurdle.

Like I said before, getting through the wall and out of the cells was a landmark moment. This was the next hurdle. We managed the first issue; we were damn sure not going to give up now.

Chapter Seventeen

We made our way back through the narrow service tunnel and took the slow, painful return to our cells via the removed vents. That night, I lay in bed with a million ideas running through my head. We would need some food and water, too. We would need someone who could meet us on the outside to get us as far away from the prison as possible in the shortest amount of time. Would it be best to head straight for the border? How long would we have from leaving the complex and getting picked up until they realized we had gone? With any luck, say maybe four hours? Could we get to the border in that amount of time? It was possible. We would need some fake driver's licenses to cross the border. Did we know anyone who had a line on a high-quality forgery?

There was a lot of planning to do, and we hadn't even found a one-hundred-percent way out yet. We would, though. I was convinced of that. I didn't have a clock in my room, but it had to have been well after 3 a.m. before I finally fell asleep.

The next morning after breakfast, Trey and I talked with Milo about our findings. As it happened, one of Milo's buddies on the outside used to work for the City of Phoenix. He explained how to make an easy manhole cover remover using a small piece of metal and some wire. It wouldn't be hard to put one together using wires from an old, broken-down lamp. We were one step closer to the next phase of our escape plan. Perfect. The future was looking brighter and brighter for us.

That afternoon, I was out in the yard with Trey and Milo. Trey had to go inside, I think, to hit the restroom? Milo and I were talking when, of all things, he suddenly stopped mid-sentence and walked away from me. What the hell? Was it something I said?

I turned around to see Tito making his way right towards us. Milo closed the gap with his left arm out to act as a buffer, keeping distance between them both. Tito grabbed Milo's left wrist and twisted it. As Milo reacted to the wrist lock, Tito hit him across the jaw with a hard jab from his left hand. Stunned, Milo went down. His noble act gave me just enough time to brace myself for Tito's onslaught.

I should have been aware that a week had passed and that Tito was now out of solitary. I should also have been aware that he would not be in a good headspace when he got out. Who knew what his beef with me was about? Right now, it didn't matter. All that mattered was staying alive.

I raised my fists and tried my best to read his hands. Chances were, he was going to come at me with a wild right. If you think about it, most street brawls start with a wild right. I guess they figure if they get lucky with that first shot, the fight will be over before it even begins.

Seeing me raise my fists, he got into a boxing stance and started circling me. I kept moving, staying out of reach of his right hand. He wasn't smiling now. In fact, he was very pissed off. In some ways, fighting a guy who is pissed off can work to your advantage, as when they are angry, they are not calm, and when they are not calm, they tend to make mistakes.

I peppered Tito with some jabs, partly to help me gauge the distance between my hands and his face, and partly to keep him away from me. He threw a couple of rights that I managed to block, and I continued to circle him. Tito then switched it up, unleashing a flurry of left-hand jabs at my face. One clipped me just enough on the jaw to make my legs wobble. Not good.

As I staggered and tried to correct my balance, he lunged at me. Seeing him drop his guard, I let fly with an uppercut. Trust me, it was a lucky shot. I had never been a master of uppercuts, crude, but effective. Some of Tito's teeth went flying out of his mouth like peppermint Tic Tacs. He spat blood, too. I think it took his brain a moment to register what had happened to him.

I didn't hesitate. In his confusion, I grabbed his head with my left hand and punched him repeatedly with my right. He went to the ground. I tried to step back to distance myself from him, but at the last second, he got hold of my right leg and pulled me down with him. The prisoners watching cheered, probably the most entertainment they'd had all month.

He raised his right arm to try to punch me. Using my left leg, I kicked him in the face repeatedly with the heel of my foot. I guess it was right around then that the alarm sounded. One of the watchtower guards must have seen the commotion and hit the panic button. Everyone on the yard dropped to their bellies in the dirt. Tito made one more attempt to get me. I heard a shot ring out, and moments later, one of the prisoners lying near us howled in pain. He had been shot. Life was cheap in this hellhole.

Tito finally gave up trying to fight me. I definitely felt I had shown him I was the superior fighter, but at what cost? A month in the hole? I would soon find out as the guards sprinted toward us.

Chapter Eighteen

Apparently, it took them hours to clear the yard. Milo, Tito, and I were taken to the hole. Everyone else was taken back to their cells. I heard later that our entire wing was on lockdown after this, and people were pissed at Tito. Sunday evening ruined. Dinner in their cells. He would be a marked man after this. Luckily, word spread that Milo and I were not at fault here.

I ate in my cell and resigned myself to at least a week in solitary. Back to the mindless routine: working out, pacing back and forth. I tried to see it as "quiet time." Our wing was always so noisy. At least in here, you could sit in silence and reflect on your life. I had never meditated before, but I wondered if this was the way to survive isolation.

Surprisingly, I actually slept pretty well that night. I had held my own against Tito and given him a good battering. My name and reputation behind the walls was good. I was no coward and I was handy with my fists. Sounds stupid now, but in prison that sort of thing counts for a lot.

The next day, I ate breakfast when it was served and contemplated my forthcoming workout. Before I could get started, I was interrupted by two guards who told me to face the wall and cuff up. I was being taken away. Back to my cell, I foolishly hoped.

Nope, wrong direction. From what I could tell, I was being taken to the administration building. Was I finally getting out of here? I doubted it. Unless one of the Feds finally did the right thing and pulled some strings to get me released. I know, foolish hopes. But one can dream, eh?

Yeah, I was right, the administration building. The two guards took me to a small holding cell and told me to "sit tight." Yeah, right, like where was I going to go with my hands cuffed behind my back? A nice casual stroll down Main Street? I wish.

They didn't keep me waiting long. The same two guards who brought me there reappeared about five minutes later. Trust me, a five-minute wait is a blessing in prison. These guys think nothing of keeping you waiting two, three, or even four hours. I mean, granted, it's not like I had anything else to do, but it still feels pointless when they drag you out and make you wait half a day.

The guards got me up off my seat, and each grabbed an arm. We left the holding cell, walked down the hall, and turned a corner. One of them grabbed a door handle and looked at me.

"They're ready for you now, Raines."

Ready? They? Who were they? And was I meant to be prepared for this? Nice to give me some forewarning, fellas. I was walking into a room totally unprepared for what faced me.

I walked into a room that looked like a judge's chambers. In front of me sat a guy I had never seen before, wearing an expensive suit and looking like a serious prison administrator. The captain, I was soon to learn, and the warden, whom I had met briefly on my first day behind the wire.

The warden told my guards to uncuff me, which they did. I rubbed my wrists to get the blood circulating again.

"Take a seat, please, Mr Raines," instructed the captain.

"Thanks," I replied, sitting down. I felt like I was about to get interrogated.

"So we are conducting an investigation into the unfortunate events that happened on Sunday in the recreation yard," started the captain. "Do you have anything to say on the matter?"

Now, I personally had a lot to say on it. I could have said I had never done anything to piss off or annoy Tito Sandoval, and that he was picking on me completely unprovoked. If I had been left free rein, I probably would have killed him or seriously hospitalized him for being so aggravating. However, prison rules dictated that any form of statement, any form of whining, complaining, or even just telling the truth about what actually happened, would be considered "snitching." The prisoners' rules were more important to them than those set by the authorities. I had no choice but to follow them and say nothing.

"Not really," I finally replied. "From what I remember, Tito accidentally fell down, and as he lost his balance, he took me down by accident."

The man in the suit looked at the warden, then at the captain. They all knew it was nonsense. In fact, they probably had the whole thing recorded.

"Okay, Raines. So that's how you want to play it?" asked the captain.

"I wish I could say more. Anything to help you, fellas, out?" I lied.

"Uh-huh," said the warden.

"Last chance, Raines," said the captain.

"Sorry, Captain. I have nothing more to add on the matter," I replied.

"Very well then," said the captain, looking over to the warden.

"Prisoner Raines," started the warden. "As you know, I pride myself on running a no-nonsense, incident-free prison. This is the second incident in ten days involving you and Prisoner Sandoval."

"Eight days," corrected the captain.

"Ah, yes, eight days. Regardless, you see my point, Raines. I cannot have you two going at it like savages. In fairness to you, my understanding is you have not been the instigator in any of these events."

I didn't say anything, but I did nod in agreement. Even a gesture like this is seen as snitching in some prisons. Whatever, so sue me.

"However, I cannot afford to have any further disruptions to Coyote Ridge. You have left me no choice but to transfer you out of your wing. These men will escort you back to your cell to collect your belongings, and you will serve out the rest of your time on C Wing."

Transferred? What? C Wing? I was gobsmacked. I did not see this coming at all. There had to be some mistake. The old fart even admitted that I was not the guilty party here. So why was I being punished? I had to say something. But what?

Chapter Nineteen

"If I haven't done anything wrong, why am I being transferred?" I asked the warden.

"We are actually transferring both of you," the captain replied, "as per prison policy. You can't remain, as we do not know how many of his friends are still on your wing. We would be leaving you open to retaliation if we left you in D Wing."

"So there is no chance of me coming back to D Wing at a later date?" I asked.

The captain thought for a moment. "It's not impossible, but chances are improbable."

Very cryptic, I thought. The way he was speaking, I was likely not to be coming back to D Wing. I wondered if I could start making escape plans again from C Wing and somehow meet the guys deep inside the old prison. There had to be a way to get a message to Trey.

The warden gave a final rah-rah speech about rewarding good behaviour and all that blarney. I played the role of the good little convict, "Yes, sir, no, sir. Very good, sir." Finally, I was cuffed up again and escorted back to D Wing to collect my measly belongings.

For the entire journey back to my cell, my mind kept racing over possible options to continue our escape plans. Goddamn Tito had done this. He was to blame. Rule number one in prison: MIND YOUR OWN BUSINESS. Tito had not done so, and now he was messing up my life more than he would ever know. Somehow, some way, I would get my revenge on that guy. He would pay for this. With any luck, I will be out of here in a few weeks. Perhaps I could wire some money from Mexico to one of the guys (Milo?) so someone can give him a bit of, well, let's say, "counselling." One that would put him in the prison hospital for a month. That would teach him. For now, I had to keep calm, get a message to Trey, and start working on an escape plan from C Wing.

There were about two dudes on the floor when we entered D Wing. Unfortunately, neither of us knew by name. I am sure, given how communication works in prison, that Trey and Milo would get the message. These two guys would see me escorted away, and by the time all the guys got back from their day jobs, the entire wing would know.

The guards marched me up the stairs to the third tier. When we got to my cell, they uncuffed me.

"You've got two minutes. Move it," the taller of the two guards said to me.

"What about my painting supplies?" I asked.

"Just leave them," said the shorter guard.

Fine. It probably only took me one minute to grab what few material possessions I had in this cell. I would have to somehow get a message to Trey and start again from ground zero in clawing my way out of this hellhole.

I had everything tossed into my drawstring laundry bag and returned it to the guards.

"So we're going to cuff you, but in front so you can hold your bag," explained the shorter guard.

"Yeah, that's fine," I said, holding out my wrists ready for the painful steel cuffs to be put back on.

The shorter guard slapped the cuffs back on. Thankfully, then he used his key to loosen them up so the tempered steel wasn't cutting into my wrist bones anymore. Be thankful for small mercies on the inside. I tell ya.

The pair then marched me back down the stairs. I really wish this had been Sunday so I could have gotten word to Trey or Austin. God knows how long they planned to hold Milo in isolation. With any luck, they would let him out at some point today.

We left D Wing and headed back into the administration building. The guards led me through twists and turns inside until we reached an exit door with a sign indicating it led to C Wing. I had never been to this part of the prison complex before, and I was madly trying to keep some sort of mental map of the way we had come. All my life, I had a pretty good sense of direction. You could put me in just about any town and within minutes I would figure out which way was north, south, east, etc. I was not 100 percent confident, but I was fairly sure we were now heading west. Which would mean D Wing was somewhere to the south. If I got any yard time today, I figured I might be able to check the sun's position to confirm my guesses.

As we exited the admin building, I felt the sun on my back. I was right. We were heading west. Good to know the internal GPS in me still worked. This would be important to remember as I tried to tunnel out of C Wing and meet up with the guys soon. I still had hope.

I could see the C Wing building ahead of me. Here we go again, I thought. At least now I was well-versed in prison politics. No one would look at me and think of me as a new fish. There is something in the way a new guy carries himself that hardened crims pick up, body language, or whatever it is called. The way you walk, the way you carry yourself, the way you hold your head. All of that is assessed in seconds. I felt confident.

We entered C Wing. Immediately, I noticed it looked like newer construction inside, unlike D Wing. Only two levels as well. Was that good? Fewer guys, I guessed. So, probably good.

Once again, I was taken up to the top tier. This could be good. I assumed the ground-level tier would be harder to burrow out of. I was towards the far end of the upper level, another good sign. The further from the stairs and guards, the better. This wing had full steel doors with hatches up top for the guard to look through, plus a second hatch midway down. I assumed that was for passing through food trays and possibly cuffing you before opening the door.

"Your new home," commented the taller guard.

"Give us those wrists," said the smaller of the two guards.

I put my drawstring laundry bag down and held out my wrists. The guard undid my cuffs. I rubbed my wrists to get my circulation working again.

"Step in," said the taller guard.

I stepped in. They shut my door. I sat down and assessed my new living quarters. That's when it dawned on me. This building was all steel, not brick. No way was I getting out of this cell without power tools. I was screwed. Totally screwed.

Chapter Twenty

I spent the next few weeks in a deep depression. It was clear now, I was screwed. No hope coming. To make matters worse, C Wing was weird. No cliques here. Whatever, that didn't bother me. It was just a strange assortment of misfits and weirdos. Most people just hung in pairs, no more than three at a time. Old men, guys who had just turned 18, a big mix right across the board. There was no real racial demographic that dominated this yard either. Very different from the other wings for some reason. No, it wasn't protective custody either. I didn't understand it.

Apparently, there were two big dudes in a car who had been standing over some of the guys in here. My number one rule for surviving in prison was to mind my own business. These two hadn't hit me up; I guess they took one look at me and figured I would put up too much of a fight. Apparently, though, they were demanding money, smokes, or commissary items from some of the smaller or older inmates. You know, the "give us your Doritos each week or something bad might happen to you" type of situation.

Where was I? Oh yeah. As I said, I did my thing and kept out of other people's business. These guys were apparently putting pressure on this one skinny kid who couldn't have been more than 19. I guess he had a supportive parent-son relationship on the outside, as they had him putting $20 a week on their books. Well, I assumed they had him begging his family to do so. Seeing as he agreed to this so easily, the pair figured his family had money and started squeezing him for $50 a week each.

I guess after a few weeks of this, his family had had enough and cut him off. Now, with no money coming in and the pressure to pay up, the kid freaked. They cornered him, demanding payment, and the kid stabbed one of them. His buddy started to beat on the kid, and all of a sudden, everyone who had been threatened or extorted by the pair saw the opportunity and started to beat on both the stabbed guy and his buddy. Apparently, it was mayhem. Me? I was sitting in my cell reading a science fiction paperback, just minding my own business.

I guess finally, the guards sitting in their horseshoe outside the wing realized something was going on. Their usual policy at this stage is to wait until everyone is compliant before they enter. I guess that's for the safety of their officers. Fine, fair enough, I get it. But if you're the guy getting jumped by a gang, you want the cavalry to come right away, not when you're dead. Right?

Finally, they came in. Had to be 45 minutes after the fracas had first started. All swatted up, protective gear, helmets, shields, batons, tear gas, the whole nine yards. They tore into the guys still messing about and beat them senseless. We were going on lockdown. Everyone back in their cell, probably for a week.

Fine by me. At least I had books in my cell. As long as I had books, I was okay. I could work out in my cell, give myself a bird bath to keep clean, work out, and eat. Screw the majority of people on this wing. I would not have been seen dead with any of them in the so-called free world.

Yeah, we got a week-long lockdown. No big deal for me. It turned out that the boys who were doing their protection racket both got killed. Sometimes you can only push people so far. No great loss to me. Screw 'em.

So there I was passing the time in my cell when a custodian came by with a cart full of books. I was still reading my current paperback, but figured it would be smart to grab another book or two while the custodian was there. I mean, seriously, who knew when he would next come back, right?

I asked him if he had any action thrillers, maybe something political. You know, something by Tom Clancy or someone.

The custodian looked at me and said, "You're getting this paperback."

I looked up at the book. He was holding a Robert Heinlein novel, *Stranger in a Strange Land*, in front of my face.

Science fiction. I didn't want sci-fi.

"Got anything else?" I asked.

"Nah, you need to read this book," he insisted.

"What about those?" I asked, pointing to a stack of other books on his cart.

He sifted through them and pulled out a Michael Crichton novel.

"Here, you can get this too," he said, "But make sure you read this one cover to cover."

He slipped both paperbacks through the food tray hatch.

"Thanks," I said, although more out of courtesy than actual thanks.

I lay back down on my bunk. What a weird guy. Why would he insist I read that book? I wondered.

I flicked through the Michael Crichton novel. Okay, this had some potential.

Not really thinking about it, I picked up *Stranger in a Strange Land,* and a postcard fell out of it. Weird. Someone must have been using it as a bookmark.

I picked it up. Postcard of Tampa, Florida. Okay.

I read it. This is what it said:

"Hi JunioR, going on a trip soon. Are you coming? Regards M.A.T."

Okay, so someone called Junior is missing their postcard from someone called Mat. Big deal.

I wasn't aware of anyone on the block called Junior.

It was only a few days later that I realized what it actually meant.

Chapter Twenty-One

Talking about not being quick on the uptake. It wasn't Junior. It was JunioR. J.R., John Raines. It wasn't from someone called Mat. It was M.A.T., Milo, Austin, and Trey! How could I have been so dumb? They were sending me a coded message.

It's funny how I figured it out. I was in that weird state, that moment when you're about to fall asleep, not properly awake, but not yet asleep either. I wasn't even thinking about it, but it came to me. Why would you sign your name M.A.T. instead of Mat?

There was no way I could break out of this place without power tools. It was one thing to hack crumbly rocks in D Wing, but to cut through steel? I had no chance. I had to get a message back to Milo.

I grabbed a pencil and the postcard. I erased Milo's message to me and instead wrote my own: *Hey M.A.T. No vacation for me, sincerely JunioR.* I shoved it back into the pages of the sci-fi book the custodian had lent me. Could he be trusted to get it back to Milo and the boys? I had to assume so. I had nothing of value to pay him for the delivery.

We were still on lockdown when the book custodian returned a day later. He opened my feeding tray slot.

"Hey, bro. How was the novel?" he asked me.

"Great, thanks. You can have it back," I replied. "But I have nothing to pay you, though."

"It's okay, bro. Milo figured as much. He's got you covered," explained the custodian.

"Oh shit, thanks," I replied. Not gonna lie, I was relieved. You can get anything in prison, but, much like the so-called free world, it all costs something.

"Hey man, he also told me to tell you, he's been transferred to your old cell," the custodian added. "Hope that means something to you."

"Ah. Okay, thanks, man," I replied. "I owe ya."

He gave me another paperback to read, this one on World War II history, and said his goodbyes.

I never learned his name, but he seemed like a stand-up dude.

So Milo had my old cell. I remembered that when Trey and I told him the plan, he couldn't join in because he was based on the ground floor in D Wing. Not gonna lie, I was kind of jealous. I felt it should have been me. That said, if anyone deserved the chance to escape, specifically from my hard work, it was Milo. If I couldn't go, then he was my first choice to take my place. I wished him nothing but the best.

I wondered if they had found a way out through the sewers yet. I guess I wouldn't know about them getting free until after headcount the morning after they broke out. I wondered if they were still planning to head to Mexico, or if they had another escape route in mind. I guess I would never know now.

We were finally out of lockdown. I learned that both bullies were dead. If the guards had come in right away, at least one of them might still be alive. At the end of the day, the stark realization was this: the guards did not care if any of us lived or died. All they were concerned about was making it through their shift without getting killed. Fair enough, I get it. It was just a job to them. But still, it hit home. No one here will save you. If you live or die, thrive or survive, it is all up to you and you alone. Scary. But you know what, maybe that was the same on the outside too?

We were finally out of lockdown. Got to admit, it did feel good to be out of the cell, just for a change of scenery, ya know. Down on the floor, there were still blood stains from the two guys who had been killed. A nasty reminder: anyone can take anyone out on any given day. Stay on high alert at all times.

I wasn't great on my Cowboys and Indians history, but I was pretty sure that the famous (infamous?) outlaw Jesse James was shot in the back by the so-called Coward of the County. My point is this: no matter how badass you are, anyone can beat you if they cheat and use a sneak attack. I remained on high alert whenever I was on the floor.

Chapter Twenty-Two

So I guess I got jumped. I say I guess because I woke up in the prison infirmary with no memory of what happened. Cracked skull, swollen eye, split lip, and bruises up and down my legs and arms.

They kept me in the infirmary for a few days to make sure I didn't have a concussion, well, not a *serious* concussion. Then they stitched me up, let me rest for three days, and sent me back to C Wing and my cell.

It was only back in my wing and talking to two of the younger guys on my pier that I managed to learn what had happened.

After our lockdown, we were finally let back out of our cells. While I had been keeping myself busy, working out, cleaning my cell, reading books, and stuff like that, I wanted to take advantage of the fact that I could get out and get some sunshine and some semblance of fresh air in the rec yard.

Because C Wing was such a mixed bag of prisoners, there weren't really any cliques. Now here's the thing: being in a gang, or a semi-organised group of guys, whatever you want to call it, may seem like something out of *West Side Story*, or *The Outsiders*, you know, Socs versus Greasers and all that. But in all seriousness, it was a necessity to stay alive here. There are times when you need that extra set of eyes and ears to watch your back, or another set of fists and boots if violence kicks off.

I didn't have any of that in this yard. Pathetic, I know.

So without thinking, the moment the rec yard opened, I took the opportunity to get outside. I didn't know there was a heavy cell search going on in one of the tiers of A Wing. To stop any prisoners from running interference on their tier search, they let them all into our rec yard. What the authorities didn't know, or at least didn't factor in, was that two of the guys from that tier were Tito's boys, and Tito's boys had beef with a certain someone. That certain someone being me.

Apparently, from those who witnessed it, I had walked ahead of the others on our wing and was deep in thought. Tito's two goons spotted me, figured out who I was, and bum-rushed me. Kind of my fault. Kind of their fault. I should have been on high alert. I should have been carrying a weapon.

Prison weapons, usually shanks, were seen as highly illegal by the authorities. If they caught you with a weapon, you faced another one to fifteen years tacked onto your sentence. No one wanted that. However, in most prisons, being caught by your enemies without a weapon could earn you a death sentence. Which would you choose? To go unarmed and face getting shanked to death? Or to be armed and get caught and earn yourself more time in the joint? Neither option appealed, obviously. But as I said earlier, there were two sets of rules in here: one set by the warden and guards, and the other set by the prisoners. Guess which set most prisoners followed?

You guessed it. The prisoners' rules were more important than the authorities' rules.

As I recovered from the assault, the question became: how do I reach out and get revenge on Tito and his boys? To do nothing would be seen as a weakness. To do nothing would probably invite others to try to attack me further down the road. I had no way of getting into their wing. I had no way of getting at Tito or them. Of course, if they ever got put back on our rec yard again, then it would have to be S.O.S., smash on sight.

Until that moment came, I had no idea how to "get at" these fools. I guess that opportunity would come in due course. The saying "revenge is a dish best served cold" made a lot more sense now. Their day would come, and Tito would pay for what he had done to me. That was for sure.

It had been just over a week since I'd been jumped. I was slowly recovering. The stitches in the back of my head had dissolved, and most of the bruising on my arms and legs had faded. I was still stiff and sore, but nowhere near as bad as when I first came to in that hospital bed. I tell you something, getting into fights, or I guess I should say getting beaten up, in your late forties was a lot worse than getting beaten up at 17. At 17, you get beaten up, two days later, you're good to go. As you get older, it takes longer and longer to recover. I guess at a certain age, once you get beaten up, you *don't ever really recover properly.*

So yeah, it had been just over a week. It was well past lights out on the wing when I was woken up by what sounded like gunshots. Sound was weird in our cells; you could swear a noise came from, say, the south, but in reality, it had come from the north, and it just bounced off all the different buildings and confused you.

I listened for more noise but didn't hear any more shots. I did hear what sounded like a bunch of guards running around on our wing. I stayed awake a little longer, listening, but eventually fell back asleep.

The next morning, I was up at 5 am, cleaning my cell and getting ready for head count before chow. No one opened our doors. What was going on? Eventually, a custodian came by with a tray of breakfast food. He told me we were back on lockdown. Something had definitely kicked off last night. I guess I would have to wait until lockdown was over to find out what had happened.

That afternoon, lockdown was lifted.

That afternoon, I found out what had happened last night.

It wasn't good. Not good at all.

Chapter Twenty-Three

Wow. I just got word. Milo and Trey are dead. I am stunned. I am shocked. I am at a loss right now. How did this happen? In the afternoon, they finally let us out of lockdown.

I was heading to the chow hall to get some dinner when someone slipped me a kite. A kite is a message from one prisoner to another, usually written on a tiny piece of paper and handed to you. This was one of the main ways guys exchanged information, especially between different wings of the same prison. Sometimes, even from the outside world to prison. Many times these could be written on minuscule pieces of paper, often in the smallest handwriting known to man.

I pocketed the kite and went to eat dinner. I didn't want to pull it out in view of the guards and get caught with it, since I had no clue what the contents of the note were. Not going to lie, after being in lockdown all morning, I was actually enjoying being out of my cell and eating with others. Weird, right?

After dinner, I actually hung out on the main floor for a while, just making small talk and watching a bit of the communal TV. Normally, I didn't waste any time with the people on the floor; I ate and went right back to my cell. Stay in my own lane. Mind my own business and all that. For some reason that night, I guess I was being sociable. I hung out and chatted with a few of the inmates in our car. Nice enough folks for the most part, perhaps I should spend more time getting to know them? The reason I bring this up is that of all the evenings to hang back and chat, it had to be this one.

So I finally returned to my cell. I was actually in a good mood for a change. I guess being on lockdown, getting out of lockdown, going back on lockdown (okay, it was just for the morning), then getting out made me appreciate the small bits of freedom we did have. The freedom to leave your cell. The freedom to eat dinner at the chow hall. The freedom to hang out and watch TV with the other inmates, etc. I guess it sounds pretty lame for those of you on the outside, but sometimes just little things like this meant so much. Someone once told me: how to be happy? Be grateful for what you have. How to be unhappy? Focus on what you don't have. Simplistic for sure, but also true in my humble opinion.

I lay back down on my bunk and started reading the paperback I was halfway through. That's when I remembered the kite that had been slipped to me on the way to the food hall. I retrieved it from my pocket and unfolded it.

"Milo and Trey are dead. Shot last night."

That's all it said. I know that many times, when parents hear bad news about one of their kids, they struggle to accept it. "No, that can't be true. I just spoke to little Jimmy one hour ago." That type of thing. As soon as I read this note, I *knew* it was all true. I *knew* it was them.

The hows and the whys? I didn't know. Well, at least not yet. I had to find out.

It HAD to be something to do with the prison break. Now I needed to locate someone who might know more about what actually happened.

I checked the time. It was 30 minutes to head count. I left my cell and headed back downstairs to the floor. The first couple of guys I spoke to were clueless. They knew nothing about why we were on lockdown this morning or the rifle shots from last night. To me, that was crazy. It just showed how unplugged-in these guys were to prison life. Prisoners gossip more than little old ladies over a shared backyard fence. Everyone knew everything about each other's business. Someone must know.

One of the old-timers had just finished watching TV. He got up from his seat and, I assume, was making his way back to his cell. I collared him.

"Hey, why were we on lockdown this morning?" I asked.

"There was a prison break in D Wing last night," explained the lifter.

"Oh shit. No way," I replied. Inside, I was thinking this is just as I had suspected.

"The guards shot them both," said the old timer.

"They try and shoot their way out or something?" I asked, which made no sense as my plan had always been to tunnel out, not to use force against the guards. Of course, they could have decided to change tactics and try to overpower some guards and shoot their way out of here. However, in my mind, that was a suicide mission doomed to failure. What had gone wrong?

"No, it's crazier than that," the old geezer explained.

"Oh. Really?" I asked.

"Yeah, somehow these two managed to dig their way out of here," said the old timer.

"No way," I exclaimed in false shock.

“Yeah. D Wing is all old concrete, no steel like here. They pretty much dug their way out.”

“Wow. That's crazy,” I added for good effect.

“So if they dug their way out, how did they get shot?” I asked.

“They came up in the middle of Red Mesa Avenue,” explained my new pal. “Apparently, there was a manhole in the middle of the street. They probably should have looked for one out of view from the watchtowers.”

Red Mesa was one of the main roads around the prison. I came in on Red Mesa Avenue when I was transported here.

“Oh shit,” I replied.

“So from what I heard,” the old timer continued, “an eagle-eyed guard spotted them. Gave them instructions to lie down. They refused. He killed one of them with the first shot. The other tried to run. He shot him, and he bled out waiting for the paramedics to arrive.”

“Dammit,” I cursed.

“Oh, did you know them?” he asked, surprised by my reaction.

“No, not at all,” I lied. “I support any of us who try and make a break for it.”

“Oh yeah, good point,” said the aging inmate. “They must have had help from the outside.”

“What makes you say that?” I asked.

“All that effort to get out just to run down the street? No way. You’d have someone nearby to pick you up,” said the old guy.

"Yeah, you got a point, brother," I replied. At that moment, the buzzer for head count went off. I had five minutes to get back to my cell before lockdown.

I thanked the old man and made my way back up the stairs. I was calm on the outside, but inside I was reeling.

Chapter Twenty-Four

I think I was in shock. I was at a loss. Although I had not known Trey and Milo as long as, say, my buddies back in Wappinger Falls, they had been good dudes. They took me under their wing and showed me the ropes on how to survive in here. Without them, I would have probably been dead by now.

Not only that, it could have easily been me as well. After all, it was my idea to break out. Okay, I know they were grown men and more than capable of making their own choices in life, but let's face it, it was my idea. I put the wheels in motion. Some of this was on me, for sure.

Had I been there with them, would I have made the same mistake? Coming up one manhole too soon? There was no way of ever knowing. One could turn oneself inside out, going over all the "what ifs" and stuff. Still, this news wrecked me. I think I fell into a deep depression. It was all hitting me at once. My friends were gone. Maybe I was to blame? Would they have still been alive if I had accepted my fate and not tried to break out? I didn't know. As they say, sometimes not knowing is worse than knowing.

I retreated further and further into myself. Outside of hitting the chow hall for food and leaving my cell three times a week to shower, I stayed in my cell. I read and read and read. I retreated into books. Think about it, you can pick up this small package of cardboard and paper and be transported back to World War II Europe.

You can travel back in time. A good book can take you into outer space. You read the words, and your mind transports you there. Screw the outside world, and screw this prison.

I made up my mind at that point. If I couldn't get out of here, then dammit, I wasn't going to be part of it either. I would just stay in my cell and read for the rest of my life. Screw these people. On the whole, most of them were low-life scum. Screw these guards. Screw the prison's administration staff. F, em all. Count me out. No more. I was done caring. I was done trying to fit in. I was done trying to be part of it. They could all go to hell as far as I was concerned.

As the months rolled on, I could feel my mental health slipping. I was not in a good way. I was probably only showering once a week. I wasn't working out. I was barely eating. I no longer cared. I think I lost the will to keep pushing on. I was losing it.

So there I was, sitting in my cell, totally withdrawn from everybody and everything. I was done. I was deeply engrossed in a book, just minding my own business like I had been doing for the past three months, when I heard someone come up to my cell. Then I heard a voice.

"There he is," said the voice. I didn't even bother looking up from my novel.

For all I knew, it could be someone sent to beat me up, or worse, kill me. You know what? Fuck it. Just kill me. Put all my problems behind me. Send me to the afterlife, as I was sure as shit sick of this life. You would be doing me a favor. Death's sweet release. Bring it on. I was over this life. Maybe the next one would be better? I could start again with a clean slate. A do-over? Yeah. That's what I needed.

Chapter Twenty-Five

"That's the one I want," said the voice.

Curiosity got the best of me, and I looked up to see an older dude flanked by two guards looking into my cell. Who the fuck was this guy?

"You sure?" asked one of the two guards.

"Yes, completely," said the old geezer.

"Prisoner Raines," said the other guard, "Prisoner Patterson has requested that you come and work in the metal shop."

"Can I say no?" I asked.

"Well, you can, but you would be missing out," said the old guy.

"Prisoner Raines," said the original guard, "this is a coveted position, and for some reason, Henry here thinks you are the man for the job. Opportunities like this are few and far between in this facility. You won't get a second chance."

I don't know what came over me, but for some reason I instinctively said, "Yes."

I was not looking for a prison job. I wasn't in the mood to leave my cell. I knew next to nothing about welding and metalwork, and I had no clue why this geezer chose me. But for whatever reason, I said yes. Weird.

"So, you good, Henry?" asked the taller of the two guards.

"Yeah, I'm good," said the old man. The two guards walked away, leaving the old timer by my cell.

"You mind if I come in?" he asked.

"Sure, man. Come in," I said.

"I'm Henry," he explained, extending his hand for me to shake.

I grabbed it and shook. He had a firm handshake.

"My name is John," I replied. "John Raines."

"Nice to meet ya, John," said Henry.

"So let me ask you a question," I said.

"Ask away," Henry replied.

"Why me? Why did you choose me?"

"You're a biker, right?" said Henry.

"Well, I was. Not anymore," I replied glumly.

"Well, you were. That means you have more mechanical aptitude than 95% of the guys in here," Henry explained.

"Hm. Probably," I replied.

"Besides, you're not doing anything with your time. You're just sitting in here wasting away," said Henry.

"Well, no," I replied, "I'm in here reading books and minding my own business."

Not gonna lie, Henry was starting to piss me off.

"Yeah, well. You can read books and mind your own business when the day is done. Trust me, son. You need something to occupy your mind."

"Is that so?" I asked.

"Yeah, it is so. The way I see it: you don't work out, your muscles wither away. If you don't work out your brain, your brain withers away. Use it or lose it," said Henry.

"Look, I have been around bikes most of my life," I replied, "but I've never done any fabrication or welding. I have zero experience in that stuff."

"No biggie. You can learn. I am going to train you," Henry replied.

"Okay. So what's the catch? I have to give you one hundred packets of Top Ramen or something?"

"No, no, no," said Henry. "Nothing like that."

"Because I'm telling you, I have nothing. No family and no money coming in," I replied. "I won't be able to pay you, and I don't intend to get into debt with anyone. No offense."

"You got me all wrong, John. We will be paying you. Pay starts at 35 cents an hour and goes up from there," said Henry.

"Oh," I replied. 35 cents an hour on the outside would be laughable. But in here, it was something.

"So when do we start?" I asked.

"Tomorrow morning, right after breakfast," said Henry. "Does that work for you?"

"Let me check my schedule," I joked. "Yeah, that should be good."

"Figured as much," laughed Henry. "Got any further questions for me?"

"I'll think of some," I replied.

"Very well then, John," said Henry. "If you need to find me, I am on the ground floor, at the far end. Cell C1."

"Okay, cool," I replied.

My brain, and my mistrust of everyone in here, was still trying to figure out Henry's angle. I mean, the guy didn't know me from Adam, yet he chose me to train up in the metal shop. What did he see in me that I didn't see?

Turns out, I would soon find out.

Chapter Twenty-Six

Sure enough, right after chow the next morning, I found Henry. The metal shop was a small building off the rec yard that I had assumed was some sort of utility shed for the guards, or something. I noticed that the guards had trusted Henry with the key.

I looked around the shop. Some equipment looked familiar to me; most did not.

"So where do we start?" I asked.

"Well, I was thinking to get you started on MIG welding first," explained Henry. "It's the easiest to learn and is widely used."

"Oh, okay," I replied. I had heard of MIG and TIG welding, but could not, for the life of me, explain the difference between them.

Henry ran through some safety procedures and protective gear. Stuff like welding helmets, leather heat-resistant gloves, flame-resistant aprons, and things like that. In the past, my mind would have glazed over during boring safety talks, and then I'd end up paying the price for ignoring my teacher (story of my life). So this time I made sure to pay full attention to what the old timer had to say.

The next thing Henry did was teach me the three basic tenets of MIG welding. It turned out to be distance, angle, and movement.

Apparently, it was important to pay attention to the distance from the surfaces you wanted to weld. Too close and you would burn your wire right back into the contact tip. Henry explained that half an inch to three-eighths of an inch was ideal. He had me do multiple dry runs, picking out an imaginary surface and running my torch back and forth over the area I intended to weld. He had me use my left hand on its side to help keep my torch at the recommended distance until he was satisfied I could do it right.

The next basic I had to learn was the angles at which you held your torch. Henry explained that, on a T-joint, you would want to hold your torch at a 45-degree angle, whereas on a "butt" joint, you would hold it more at a 90-degree angle. Again, Henry made me do a bunch of dry runs. He explained that for now, we would be practicing on the bench, but in the real world, you might have to weld something upside down or on its side. Master the basics and then worry about the tricky stuff. The other angle technique I had to master was the travel angle. Imagine you are welding a flat surface. The travel angle is the direction your torch moves in, away from you or towards you (pushing or dragging). Henry told me the optimum angle for travel was right around ten degrees.

So basically, I had to be mindful not to hold the torch too near or too far away from my welding site, make sure I was holding it at either a 90-degree or a 45-degree angle, and then move it at a 10-degree angle either towards me or away from me. It seemed like a lot to remember.

I thought back to learning to ride a motorcycle. In those early days, it was a conscious decision to hold the clutch in, flick up with your boot to change gears, then slowly let out the clutch. It felt like I would always have to focus 100% to change gears, but within weeks, it became an extension of my body. I didn't even think about it. I was hoping I could get like that in time with welding.

Like most skills, you start slow. Then, ever so slowly, you build up speed. Slow is smooth, and smooth is fast.

The third and final basic Henry taught me that day was travel speed, which was how fast you pushed or dragged your torch while welding. Too slow, and the bead would be too wide. Too fast and your bead would be too narrow. On top of travel speed, there was also the movement as you welded, which he called "manipulation." You could weave, zigzag, or do a small curling motion. Once again, he had me practice dry runs until I started to get the movements and tempo right.

After that, Henry had me set my MIG welder to the settings on the chart posted on the wall of the metal shop. The settings were based on the thickness of the scrap metal and the wire diameter. He explained that for now it was more about learning technique, and in time we could fine-tune everything.

After my introduction to MIG welding, we had a coffee break, just like in a real auto shop. Although my brain was spinning with everything I needed to remember, I was enjoying it. Henry was a cool old timer, and it did me good to get the old brain cells firing again. Reading books was fine, but Henry had been right. I needed to get out of my cell and stimulate my mind.

After the break, Henry had me set up at one of the welding benches. He grabbed a pile of scrap metal and laid it out. Standing next to me, he watched me set everything up and run through a couple of dry runs before hitting the trigger. Once he was satisfied I had my distance, angle, and movement for a basic butt weld locked down, he told me to make my first attempt. I was kind of nervous. I did my best to recall everything he had told me. In the back of my mind, I knew it was going to take time, but you had to start somewhere.

Henry watched over my shoulder for the first few attempts, gave me a few pointers, and then told me to continue. He left me a stack of small scrap metal pieces to work on while he got busy on the other side of the shop.

You cannot rush experience; you have to earn the hours you put in. Time and time again, I practiced the basic techniques Henry had shown me. I was so focused that I nearly jumped when he tapped me on the shoulder.

"Hey, big guy. Come on. It's time for lunch. Plenty of time for more of that when we get back," he said.

I shut everything off, removed my protective gear, and followed Henry out to the chow hall. I ate my lunch in silence, trying to visualise everything he had taught me: distance, angle, movement. Distance, angle, movement. There could have been twenty prisoners with shanks behind me, and I would have been oblivious. All I could think about was welding.

We returned after lunch and continued working. Henry had me at it all afternoon. Around 4:45 p.m., he stopped and reviewed my attempts.

Some beads were too thin, some too thick. One weld, he pointed out, had been too long of an arc, and there were small holes I hadn't noticed. All in all, he was a good teacher. He took time to explain what I had done wrong and how to improve the next day.

He had me clean the shop from top to bottom before we wrapped up.

I tell ya, I slept like a baby that night. Even though there was no heavy lifting or anything, I was wiped out by the time I hit my bunk. It felt great, ya know?

Chapter Twenty-Seven

That Saturday morning, after breakfast, I was sitting in my cell, reading a book (of course) and minding my own business. I could hear someone coming up the stairs. I listened with one ear as they approached and kept reading. That person stopped at my door.

"You ready?" asked the person.

I recognized the voice immediately; it was Henry.

"Ready? I thought the shop wasn't open on the weekends?" I asked.

"It's not. Today we do laps around the rec yard, son," Henry replied.

"Oh," I said. "I thought I would stay in and read. Work on my brain."

"Hey, son. Listen up. The best way to work on your brain power is to walk," Henry replied. "That's a proven fact."

"Well, I don't know about that," I replied.

"It is!" insisted Henry. "Besides, you gotta get your cardio in. So get off your lazy ass and let's get moving, Raines."

"Alright, alright. Gimme two minutes," I replied. "Meet ya downstairs."

Henry left me to take a piss and brush my teeth. I hurried down to the ground floor, where I saw him talking to another old geezer.

"Ready?" I said to him. He said goodbye to his friend, and we walked together out to the yard.

Henry asked me how I liked working in the metal shop.

"Yeah, man, it's been really good. I enjoy it much more than I thought I would," I replied.

"Being a biker, I knew you would," Henry beamed.

"I do. Trust me," I replied. "However..."

"There's always a however," Henry responded.

"Look, I am super grateful for everything you have done for me. I am super grateful you're taking the time to train me. But let's face facts here. I'm under no illusion that I will ever get out of here. I have accepted my fate. Pretty sure I will end up dying in here. Maybe it would be best to spend your time teaching someone younger? Someone who is only inside for a year or two?"

"Let me stop you right there," said Henry. "First off, you've got no idea when you're getting out. I've seen guys facing 20 years get let out. New Arizona governor comes in. The new president takes power. You never know. Occasionally, some hotshot special agent gets caught doing something dirty, and they look into old cases. Then everyone gets let go. You never know. So strike that thought from your mind."

"Uh, okay. I didn't even think of that," I replied.

"On top of that. Let's say worst case, you never get out," said Henry.

"Okay. I'll indulge you," I replied.

"Take a look around you," Henry said, waving his arms around the rec yard.

I saw a bunch of young guys hanging out.

"You know the one common factor all these boys have?" Henry asked me.

"No. What's that?" I asked.

"Lack of a good father figure," Henry explained. "Like most of these guys, if they had a dad or an uncle in their lives to show them the way, they probably wouldn't be in here. Unless, of course, your uncle is Jesse James or someone."

"Really? All of them?" I asked.

"Most of them. Guaranteed," said Henry. "Think on this."

"Okay," I said, bracing myself for a lecture.

"In the old days, a young man would start helping his dad out around the farm as soon as he was old enough. Maybe his uncle, too, maybe some farmhands. He got to learn firsthand how to be a man. How to act. Right and wrong. Responsibility to family. All that good stuff. You follow me so far?"

"Yeah. So far so good," I replied.

"So then comes industrialization. Men leave farms to work in factories. Long hours. No father on the scene. Right?"

"Yeah, I guess," I replied.

"Then come both World Wars, and a ton of good men get killed," said Henry.

"Yeah, that's true," I said.

"After both World Wars, more and more people took desk jobs. I forget the stats, but something like 50% of families ran some form of farm in the early 20th century. By the late 1950s, I think only 3% of family farms still existed," Henry explained.

"Okay," I said.

"Then in the 1960s, divorce rates skyrocketed. Feminism, all of that stuff. In divorce courts, most of the time the woman gets custody of the kids, right?" said Henry.

"Right," I replied, thinking about my own dad, who had cut out when I was young.

"So we now have generations of men raised by women. Mothers at home, school teachers at school. Apparently, the number of male school teachers is even less now than it was in your day or my day," said Henry.

"Wow, I didn't even think of that," I replied.

"So you have generation after generation of young men struggling to find their place in society. Struggling to figure out how to behave as a man. You get it?"

"Sure," I replied.

"These guys need guys like you. Show them the path. Let them learn from your mistakes. Steer them right, John," Henry explained.

"You know, I never thought of that," I replied. Dammit, Henry was right. I had been so engrossed in my own woes that I had never thought of the others.

"So yeah. By my reckoning, you can still do a lot of good," said Henry.

"You are correct, good sir," I replied.

"Okay, here's another scenario. What are you now? 42?" he asked.

"Nah, 46," I replied.

"Okay. 42, 46, whatever," said Henry. "Let's say you do get out at age 60."

"Okay," I replied.

"You will have no savings. No retirement fund. No, nothing."

"Shit. I didn't even think about that," I replied.

"What are you going to do for work? Deal more drugs? You know how many guys just end up coming back to this shithole?" Henry asked.

"I dunno. 50%?" I asked.

"Most of them," said Henry. "However, fully skilled welders can write their own pay check on the outside."

"That's true," I replied.

"So the way I see it, you can't lose," said Henry.

"Well, you make some good points, but I never thought of it that way," I replied.

"You're welcome!" teased old Henry as we kept doing laps around the rec yard.

"Smart ass," I said.

"Quit griping and keep walking," said Henry.

Chapter Twenty-Eight

After Henry's pep talk on the yard that day, I was determined to become a master welder. Over the next year, with countless hours and long days, I practiced and practiced until I saw improvement in my welding skills. On top of that, I did everything and anything asked of me in the prison metal shop. I swept the floors, I cleaned up the place, and I repaired and maintained the power tools. I took my new responsibilities very seriously. I was like a man possessed.

In time, Henry started giving me basic welding jobs to do. He would also inspect my handiwork afterwards and make small criticisms to help me improve. After a month or two of doing those types of jobs, Henry stopped passing judgment and started complimenting me. I had arrived. I was now an official "Henry-approved" welder.

One morning, Henry came into the shop and announced, "Okay, no more welding for today."

What had I done wrong? I had thought Henry was pleased with my work performance these days.

"Something wrong?" I asked.

"No, not at all. You're ready for your next lesson," smiled Henry.

Next lesson? I thought I had mastered MIG welding. What now?

"Uh oh. What's that going to be?" I asked.

"Metal fabrication," smiled Henry. "Don't worry, it's simple to learn."

"Yeah. Says you," I replied.

"Trust me. It is. You learn by doing. Heck, with me as your teacher, you'll go far," bragged Henry.

"So you say," I said. "So how do I start then?"

"I'm going to get you to make a simple metal box, John," said Henry.

"Okay, sounds good," I said. Really, I was thinking I have no clue what I'm doing.

Henry fished about in a scrap-metal box, retrieving a small sheet of metal. He handed it to me and went to our wall of tools, grabbing some tin snips and a ball-peen hammer.

"See that vice over there?" Henry asked, pointing to the far corner of the room.

"Yeah, I see it."

"Use the tin snips, this hammer, the vice, and the block of wood and go make me a box, John."

"Um. Okay. You got it," I replied, and walked over to the other corner of the metal shop.

I thought for a moment. How do I do this?

I thought back to when I was a kid in arts-and-crafts classes. If I thought of the sheet of metal as a piece of cardboard, I could cut out tabs using the tin snips, then fold the metal by putting it into the vice.

I grabbed a marker and drew out some rough tabs. That would be where I would cut.

I looked back, and Henry was not watching me. I assumed that was a good sign. He trusted me to just get on with it.

I grabbed the tin snips and very carefully cut into the small sheet of metal. I found that if I just thought of it as a pair of scissors and a piece of cardboard, it was a lot easier to work with.

After cutting the tabs into the piece of metal, I opened the vice and placed the body of the metal in it. I clamped it down and, using the ball-peen hammer, I managed to bend one of the folds. I had actually done it. Mind blown. I then removed the piece of metal and did the other side. Success.

But how to do the folds on the short ends? Because both the long tabs were already folded over, there was no way to do the shorter bends.

Then I remembered Henry had mentioned the block of wood. What was I meant to do with that?

It suddenly dawned on me. I could put the piece of metal into the vice, hold the already-bent sheet of metal over it, and gently use the ball-peen hammer to bend the final two folds. Henry was a crafty devil. I'll give him that.

Eventually, I had made a very primitive metal box. I waited until Henry finished what he was doing and called him over.

"Hey, Henry. I think I'm done," I announced.

"Alright. Well, let me see your handiwork then, Raines," he replied.

Henry came over and took the box from my hand.

"That's a good first start," he said.

"Well, it's not exactly uniform," I stated.

"Honestly, at this stage, I was not looking for any accuracy from you. I just wanted you to get a feel for handling metal," he said.

"That makes sense," I replied.

"Now you know what you need to do?" he asked.

"What?"

"Weld these seams up," he said, pointing to the bent-up tabs.

"Ah, yeah. Good thinking," I replied.

"You see?" said Henry. "Now you're combining skills. Fabrication and welding."

Henry was a clever guy. He was also a great teacher. I had known many people over the years who were skilled and talented in their chosen fields, but could never be teachers. They could never convey everything they had learned to a newbie like me. Henry was the opposite. I was truly blessed to have known him.

Chapter Twenty-Nine

I stuck with the welding and metal fabrication. Somewhere over the months and years, I started to get good (not to brag, but yeah), this was my thing. Satisfied, I was now welding to Henry's standards, and he also started training me on TIG welding. From how Henry explained it to me, TIG welding produced higher-quality, precise welds, especially on thinner metals. It was harder to learn and definitely harder to get good at. I could see why Henry had me start on MIG welding first.

One weekend, while walking the yard with Henry (his Saturday afternoon tradition, rain or shine), he started telling me about the history of custom bike parts. I was all ears.

"You know how it all started, don't ya?" he asked me as we walked.

"What?" I replied.

"Motorcycle parts customization, John," Henry responded.

"Oh. Because guys were not happy with their stock Harleys and wanted to make them perform better. You know, go faster and stuff. Right?" I replied.

"Well, kinda," Henry said. "I was more talking about the fabrication of parts and stuff."

"Oh, okay. No idea," I said.

"Two reasons," he continued. "First, guys were trying to get rid of parts from stolen bikes. They would sand off the serial numbers and try to mod the parts to make them harder to trace."

"Ah. That makes sense," I replied. "What's the second reason?"

"Well, these days you boys have these giant mail-order catalogs. You can just flick through them, find the sissy bar or gas tank you want, send a check, and boom, you've got your parts. In the old days, we had to make the parts ourselves. Want some cool rabbit-ear handlebars? Go make 'em yourself. That's how it all started."

"Wow. I never thought of that," I replied. "That's actually really cool."

"No shit," said Henry. "And to think you're now part of that tradition. You ought to be proud of yourself, son."

"Well, I am proud to have you as a mentor, Henry," I said.

"Well, Raines, I appreciate the kind words. But you really are a good student. You know, before you came to our wing, I tried to get some of the younger guys into this. They had no desire to learn. They had no patience. That's the trouble with kids today, Raines. Everything has to be immediate. If they're not experts on their first attempt, they get frustrated and storm off. Getting good takes time."

"That's true," I replied. "Trust me. I know."

"One thing I've learned in all my years, Raines," said Henry. "You can't rush experience. You have to earn that shit."

"That's a good point," I replied. "I had never thought of that."

"Well, you make a good student," said Henry. "Do you know why?"

"Why?" I asked.

"Because you know when to shut up and listen. That's why," cackled Henry.

"Ha ha. Very funny," I replied. "I was keen to learn. That's my defence," I joked.

"Yeah. And I appreciate that," said Henry.

Chapter Twenty-Thirty

The years rolled on. I don't know about you. Well, you're young; you're not going to understand. But as you get older, the years just seem to go faster and faster. Henry had been right. I needed something more than just sitting in my cell, cut off from the world and reading books. Working with my hands was great. At the end of each day, no matter how tired or dirty you felt, there was a sense of accomplishment that you had done something with your life that day that would make a difference.

As time passed, the old warden retired. Some of the guards who were working when I first came to this joint retired. Some quit. Some just left. Who knew where? The prisoners remained the same. The new regime came in with its big ideas. No doubt the warden picked up some of these feel-good initiatives while studying at some college. New reforms were tried. Most failed. While some of these ideas might sound good in a college textbook, in the real world, they just didn't fly, especially not in a building filled with convicted felons. Most of the new initiatives and programs lasted six months until everything went back to the way it was. Ha ha.

One thing that happened during this new regime change was this: my old buddy Tito, the prick who had taken an instant dislike to me. That one. Yeah, you remember him. The one that got me transferred out of my wing. Well, ol' Tito got transferred to our wing. Now, traditionally, prison policy should have had some file, some file that made it clear ol' Tito and good ol' John Raines cannot be on the same wing. Maybe I should have said something to the guards. No chance. This was my opportunity to get revenge on that asshole.

Word spread across C Wing that Tito was up for parole. He had five more years to go on his sentence, but I guess due to changing reforms from the outside world, they were prepared to let him out early. Maybe it was budget cuts? Maybe it was prison overcrowding? Who knows? But when I heard this news, I knew I had to mess with good ol' Tito. He still had to pay for what he had done to me.

A day later, I was sitting, reading a newspaper in the communal area downstairs. I saw him walking by, so I stuck my leg out to trip him, much like we did as kids in elementary school. Trip your friends as a joke, they take a tumble, and much hilarity ensues. I stuck my foot out right as he walked by. Sure enough, he stumbled but didn't hit the floor.

He turned in fury to attack the culprit. In a microsecond, it dawned on him that it was me. For the first time ever, I saw fear in dear ol' Tito's eyes. He dropped his fists, cursed under his breath, and stormed off. An unwritten no-no in prison: you cannot let something like that go by without exacting revenge. Tito was stuck between a rock and a hard place: save face but risk losing his parole, or avenge his perceived wrongdoing and screw up getting free, or ignore it and lose the reputation he had spent the last five years building up. I know at that point, for me personally, I would ignore it and get the hell away from here. I don't think Tito had that same self-control.

The next day, I was returning from the chow hall with Henry when Tito and one of his friends were walking towards us.

I looked over at him, made eye contact, and said loudly, "PUNK BITCH."

He looked at me, horrified, then turned and scurried away. What a difference five years made. Back then, he would have launched at me before I had even said a word to him. The tables had turned, and I was enjoying myself.

"What was all that about?" asked Henry.

"It's a long story, but I may find myself going to the hole for a week or two," I replied.

Henry thought about the information I had just relayed to him.

"Okay. No worries, brother. Do what you have to do."

Every effort of mine to fluster and harass Tito failed. Don't get me wrong, it was fun to torment this guy. I still blamed him indirectly for Milo and Tito's death. My chance to avenge them all those years ago was robbed from me. Getting transferred to C Wing, I had no way of getting back at Tito then. Revenge truly was a dish served cold.

For the next few days, I watched Tito carefully. He cooked many meals in his room, ramen-based dishes and stuff. One thing I noticed was that he bought strawberry jelly from the commissary every week. That was his pride and joy. I had an idea.

I called out "sick" from work the next day. Most of the guys were off the floor and at their day jobs. I took my morning dump and, before flushing, grabbed a small piece of, well... you know, the brown stuff. I wrapped it in toilet paper and casually walked out of my cell and downstairs. There were two old-timers across the room playing cards. Even if they saw me, they knew not to snitch. I walked into Tito's cell and searched for his prized strawberry jelly.

It took me a couple of minutes, but I found it. Using a spoon, I carefully scooped off the top layer of jelly, then grabbed the piece of poop and slipped it into his jar. I then covered the poop with the jelly I had scooped out. I screwed the top back on, wiped everything down, and returned his prized condiment to its hiding place in his cell. I then casually walked out of his cell and back upstairs. Enjoy your sandwich tonight, dumbass!

Around 5 p.m., everyone returned from their day jobs. I waited for Henry to come back, and then we went to dinner together. So far, so good.

We returned to C Wing and settled in to watch some TV. I think it was one of those celebrity dancing shows. Now, in the free world, I would never have watched garbage like that for one second, but again, in prison, things are different. It was usually one of our few chances to catch attractive women on TV, given the strict limits on the channels we had access to.

To be honest, I was so engrossed in the stupid TV show that I had forgotten about the jelly caper. I was nudging Henry and making comments about the ass on the one-hit-wonder pop singer turned wannabe dancer when I heard the most unholy wail from one of the far prison cells. Yes, it was Tito's. Yes, everyone heard it, and everyone stopped what they were doing. Moments later, I heard cursing, then the sound of someone trashing their cell. All hell was breaking loose in there.

I readied myself for a fight. Moments later, Tito came running out of his cell, tears in his eyes, a nasty-looking shank in his right hand. He scanned the rec area. He spotted me amongst the cons and charged. I jumped up, ready to fight. I wanted to set him up to destroy his chance of being paroled, not get stabbed by him.

He pushed past some of the guys who had stood up to see what all the noise was about. I grabbed a magazine off the table and rolled it up tightly. It wasn't much, but used effectively, it feels like a baton hitting you. Tito was coming in fast and angry. Sounds weird, but I felt that was a good thing. An angry assailant isn't thinking clearly and is more likely to make dumb mistakes. First off, he was attacking me right out in the open, in full view of everyone. This was good. Most guys who got jumped did it in the showers or in an out-of-the-way corner of the yard, no witnesses, no cameras. That was the proper way to do it.

Tito screeched something in Spanish that I didn't catch. He swung wildly with his shank and missed. I clobbered him on the side of his face with the rolled-up magazine. I don't know what I hit, but it rocked him. He swung around to try to stick me with his shank again. Instinctively, I put my left forearm out to block his blow. His homemade knife connected. I didn't feel it at first, but all of a sudden, there was a flow of blood, my blood, all over the floor. I heard the alarms go off and the guards come running. All I had to do was avoid his knife for a few more moments, and I would be tackled to the ground by the guards.

Tito cursed me again and readied his shank for another attack. I let loose a left-handed jab to his jaw that connected. He yelped and stepped back. That sharp tap to his chin angered him more. I squared up to him, ready to counter his next move. Before I knew it, I was grabbed from behind and tossed to the floor. The cavalry had arrived! From the corner of my eye, I could see they had Tito pinned to the floor as well. Good. Bye-bye parole, asshole. Bye-bye early release. Bye-bye freedom, you dumb fuck.

Chapter Thirty-One

As expected, the guards grabbed me, cuffed me, and took me to solitary. I knew I was facing at least a week in the hole, but trust me, it was worth it. Knowing that POS had ruined his chances of parole was payback enough. His family would be so upset that he was back inside. Well, guess what? He was still alive, but Milo and Trey were not. So screw that guy. Couldn't have happened to a nicer person.

After being dumped in solitary confinement, I took stock of my arm. I had quite a big gash in my forearm where Tito had sliced me open. I put my right arm over the wound and tried to hold together the two folds of skin to clot the bleeding. It wasn't working. Would I bleed to death? Was this my payback for messing with Tito? Should I try to call for the guards? Would that be dry snitching? I didn't know. I was more concerned with passing out from blood loss than following prison protocol at that very moment.

Just as I was contemplating hitting the buzzer to call a guard, I heard someone putting keys into the door of my cell. Was I about to receive a beatdown courtesy of the boys? I braced myself for the worst.

The door swung open, and two different guards from the ones who had escorted me here greeted me.

"Turn around and face the wall," one of them instructed.

I did so and then put my hands behind my back to be cuffed.

"Watch the blood," the same voice said to his buddy.

I felt the all-too-familiar steel cuffs cut into my wrist bones (again).

"Here, slap this on him," the same voice said.

I felt a bandage of some form go over the gash in my left forearm.

"Alright, let's move prisoner Raines," said the same guard.

I was assuming they were going to take me to the warden's office for an interrogation of some form. Granted, I was the instigator in all of this, but I had no intention of incriminating myself or Tito. That was just the way things were on the inside, no confessing, no cooperation with law enforcement.

They led me out of C Wing into the cool night air. I gotta say, it felt nice to be outside at night. Sadly, it had been way too long. They took me into the building I referred to as the "admin" building, but instead of turning left after we entered it, they took me right. Was this some form of trick to scare or intimidate me?

To my surprise, they took me to some kind of medical room. Why here and not the hospital? I have no idea. I was just glad I was getting cleaned up. See, what you don't know is that half the time when guys get stabbed by shanks, it's not so much the puncture wound or slicing that hurts you, it's the infection. As crazy as it sounds, some of these shanks are carried… uh… how can I put this? Inside a guy… if you get what I'm saying. So there's all sorts of fecal matter on the blade. It's not the blood loss that messes you up. It's the infection. Gross.

The talkative guard left me in the room with his mute buddy. Moments later, a duty nurse arrived. She took one look at my arm, shot me up with some painkillers, and cleaned the wound. Once she was satisfied it was clean, she stitched me up, then wrapped my forearm in a clean bandage and handed my silent buddy two more clean packs of bandages, shrink-wrapped.

“Give these to him when he is back in his cell,” she instructed.

Then she turned to me and said, “Leave this one on overnight. In the morning, gently remove it, then clean the wound with soap and water. Pat dry and then wrap one of these new bandages back around it. Repeat just before bed as well. You got it?”

“Yes, ma’am,” I replied, grateful to have my arm cleaned and dressed.

“You gonna give me any trouble?” Mister Silence asked me.

“No, sir,” I replied.

“Alright, you know the drill. Turn around, hands behind your back,” he instructed.

I did as I was told, fully expecting to be taken back to solitary.

We left the admin building and walked the path back towards C Wing.

When I returned, the place was already on lockdown. No one was walking around. Standard procedure after a fight.

“We reviewed the tapes, and it was clear he attacked you first,” explained my guard. It was almost as if he could read my mind, wondering why I wasn’t being taken back to the hole.

My buddy undid my cuffs and handed me the clean bandages. “Here. Take ’em,” he said.

“Thanks,” I replied. Not gonna lie, I was relieved to be back in my cell.

Much later, I heard that after a month in solitary confinement, Tito was taken to A Wing, where he served out the rest of his sentence. F that guy.

Chapter Thirty-Two

The next morning, I was walking to the metal shop with Henry. The same cop who had taken me back to my cell after being stitched up was walking in the opposite direction from us.

"Hey, Raines. Over here," he said.

I looked at Henry. He nodded.

I walked over to the guard. Henry stood apart from us, just out of earshot. This was the accepted action within the prison system for this type of thing. Poor form to be seen listening in.

"Everything okay?" I asked.

"Yeah, all good here, Raines. How's your arm?" he asked.

"Still sore. Washed and changed my bandages this morning. I reckon I'll live," I replied.

"So listen," said the guard. "You ride, right?"

"Well, not any more. But back on the outside, sure. Why, what's up?" I asked.

"I just bought a bike, and I was wondering if you could make a sissy bar for me," the guard said.

"Hmm, you got a soft tail or a hard tail?" I asked.

"What's that mean?" asked the guard.

"Back of the frame. Where the rear wheel is, is that steel tubes or shock absorbers?" I asked.

The guard thought for a moment. “Shocks,” he replied.

“Okay, cool. Yeah, I can do you one. No problem.”

“So what difference does it make if it was a hard tail frame versus shock absorbers?” he asked.

“You can go much higher with a hard tail frame on your sissy bar. On a soft tail, the taller it gets, the more it wobbles about as you travel,” I explained.

“Ah, that makes sense,” he replied.

“I’ll get started today,” I said.

“Thanks, Raines. Much appreciated,” said the guard.

“No problem,” I replied. I figured keeping on the good side of the guards wouldn’t hurt. I could always squeeze him for a favor somewhere down the road. The truth was, I had never made a sissy bar before. I had installed many a prefabricated one, but never made one from scratch. I was sure, with Henry’s help, it wouldn’t be too hard.

“Hey, so I never introduced myself. Sargent Phelps,” he said, sticking out his hand.

“Nice to meet you. John Raines,” I replied, shaking his hand.

We shook for a moment before saying our goodbyes.

“Oh, one more thing,” I said.

“What’s that, Raines?” asked Sargent Phelps.

“What sort of bike did you buy?” I asked.

“Oh, 2004 Honda Shadow,” Phelps replied.

“Do you know what model?”

“Uh… Shadow Spirit, I think,” said Phelps.

"That's a cool first bike," I responded. "Can't go wrong with those. Super reliable motor and lots of ways to customize."

"Oh shit. You know all this stuff, don't you?" he said.

"I guess so," I said before returning to Henry.

"Everything okay?" asked Henry as we continued towards the metal shop.

"Yeah. That guard wants me to make him a sissy bar for his new bike," I explained.

"That's cool. I can show you today how to do that," Henry replied.

"Oh, good. That was going to be my next question," I laughed.

"No problemo," Henry replied. "It's relatively easy. Do you know what size?"

"Well, it's a soft tail, so it's not going to be super tall," I said.

"That's damn straight," said Henry as we reached the metal shop.

True to his word, Henry had me fabricate a sissy bar in a couple of hours. We set up a makeshift jig on one of the benches. Then Henry got busy creating a centre line and mapping the bend points. We grabbed some half-inch diameter steel tubing, heating the metal with an oxy-acetylene torch before bending it around our bend points. When it was all done and ready to work on, Henry had me weld on some mounting tabs to finish it off.

By the end of the day, our piece of art was ready for Sargent Phelps.

"You know we're going to have to have him come and collect it," stated Henry.

"Oh yeah. I didn't think of that," I replied. Neither of us could be seen carrying a large metal contraption through the prison without getting reprimanded. I would have to tell Phelps about it and have him come collect it. Regardless, I think he would be pleased with our efforts.

I didn't see Sargent Phelps for the rest of the evening. I did see him the next morning, pretty much around the same place we had run into him the day before. I told him it was ready to be picked up, and he told Henry and me he would swing by after his shift.

Sure enough, just before we were about to leave for our designated lunch break, Sargent Phelps turned up.

"Knock knock," he said as he walked in.

I looked up to see him standing in the door of the metal shop. Henry went over and greeted him. As older guys and trusted custodians (well, more Henry than me), most days we were left alone in the shop, unsupervised. Getting older had some perks, I guess.

Henry made small talk with Phelps as I retrieved his newly made sissy bar and brought it over to the pair.

"Is this it?" he asked.

"Yes, sir," I replied.

"Goddamn! You guys did an incredible job," he was beaming. "Thanks so much."

"Any time," Henry replied.

"You're welcome," I said.

As he was turning to leave, he looked back at Henry and said, "I'm going to install this this weekend. I think I'll take you up on the offer. Thanks again."

We said our goodbyes. After we were sure Sargent Phelps had left, I turned to Henry and asked,

"What offer?"

"I told him to bring his scoot in, and we can customize it for him," said Henry.

"No shit," I replied. "Really?"

"Yeah," said Henry.

"Did you discuss what he would pay us?" I asked.

"Oh no. We're going to do it for FREE," said Henry.

"Free?" I was incredulous. We could make good money doing this.

"Yeah, FREE," said Henry. "The way I see it, we do all this work on spec. We see a lot more than a few bucks on the back end. Come on, John. Think. What we can score in favors from Phelps is worth more than a few bucks' worth of ramen noodles from the commissary."

"Yeah. Shit. I didn't think of that," I replied.

"So yeah. He's going to bring his bike in, and we're gonna turn it into a chopper," smiled Henry.

"We are?" I asked.

"Yeah, we can make the gas tank, handlebars, and hard-tail it here," said Henry. "He might have to purchase a few parts we can't make here, though. I'll give him a list."

"Like what?" I asked.

"Basic stuff, longer clutch and brake cables, hand grips, etc."

"Ah, yeah. Makes sense," I replied.

"Ready for lunch?" asked Henry.

"Yeah. Let's go," I replied.

Chapter Thirty-Three

Sure enough, the very next week, Sargent Phelps brought in his stock Honda Shadow with his newly installed sissy bar.

"Here ya go, boys. Feel free to do what you want to her," said Phelps.

"Don't worry, Sarge," said Henry. "We will take the best care of her."

After Sargent Phelps had left, I turned to Henry and asked, "Right. What's the plan here?"

"You're gonna strip her down. We're gonna make new handlebars. I'm going to show you how to fabricate a peanut-style gas tank. We're going to remove the shocks and hard-tail it," Henry explained.

"Oh. Okay. Cool," I replied.

"We can't make a springer front end with our limited tools, but we can machine some fork extensions," said Henry. "That will help with the whole old-school chopper look."

"Oh shit. Nice," I replied. "What about that stock kickstand?"

"I've got some ideas," said Henry with a wink. "We can do that too."

With a rough plan in Henry's brain, we got started on Sargent Phelps' bike. Well, I say "we," but it was me who stripped it down as Henry got on with his other duties.

Over the next few weeks, we worked on Phelps' bike whenever we had a spare moment. Of course, we still had regular maintenance duties across the prison, welding, fabrication, creating, and replacing parts for blown-out machines in the other prison industries. But other than that, we spent every moment building from scratch parts for his Honda.

I made my first set of handlebars. I wanted to have a go at making rabbit ears, but Henry had envisioned a set of buckhorn handlebars for this build. He figured that suited the '60s retro chopper aesthetic much better. Who was I to argue with the mad genius?

After that, we cut the rear end of the frame and hard-tailed the scoot. It would have been better with a springer front end, but hey, Sargent Phelps was a relatively young guy; his back wouldn't need a springer for a few more years, by my reckoning.

Next, Henry had me build a chopped rear fender that fit with the flow of the seat and the previously built sissy bar. After that, Henry helped me create the peanut tank that was so popular with those San Francisco-style choppers that came out of the Bay Area in the 1960s.

We only had black and red paint in the metal shop, so that's the color scheme his freshly built tank and rear fender received.

Henry got some tubing, an oxy torch, and a vice, and crafted a super-stylish brand-new kickstand. I gotta say, I was kind of jealous. I never had one like that out in the free world.

After that, Henry created six-inch fork extensions that gave the front end a traditional chopper look. Even though, in the grand scheme of things, six inches isn't that much, it effectively changed the stance of his bike so much that it was no longer a "dad" bike and was now a "rad" bike.

We contemplated creating a "cocktail shaker" exhaust for his pipes, but in the end, we had to leave them stock.

After about six weeks, we had finally done it. The bike looked certifiably badass. There was something to be said about customizing a stock bike to make it yours. No matter where Sargent Phelps traveled now with this bike, it would stand out from the pack. After all, these were custom hand-crafted pieces, not something you bought from a mail-order catalog and bolted on.

The next morning, we saw Sargent Phelps in the hall. I told him to swing by after his shift, and he was all smiles. He knew what it meant.

When we got to the shop, we rolled his bike into the middle of the floor and threw an old dusty tarp over it to make a big show of it, the "grand reveal."

Phelps turned up right before lunchtime with two of his prison guard buddies. He was like a little kid on Christmas Day. Seeing the tarp thrown over his scoot just added to his anticipation. Seeing his face when we ripped off the tarp and showed him his rebuilt bike? Priceless.

Even though he was a prison guard and we were convicts, it gave me a great sense of pride to see how happy he was with the work we did for him.

Chapter Thirty-Four

I just realized I was turning 50 in a few days. Crazy. That meant I had already done nearly 10 years in this shithole. Time really does move faster when you are an adult. I remember being a kid. The school holidays would last for eternity! Every day was an adventure that never ended.

We would stay out until the streetlights came on, then it was time to head home for dinner. My friends and I would ride our bicycles all over town. If only our parents knew what sort of craziness we got up to, exploring abandoned buildings, jumping off rocks into a lake, all sorts of shenanigans. I remember one time we found this abandoned mental hospital. One of the guys dared me to go inside. Now, I'm not a particularly superstitious person, but I tell you, I made it to the window of that hospital and got chills up my spine. Some serious bad vibes associated with that building. You could feel them. No, seriously, I could. No way was I going in there. I admitted defeat. The guys all laughed and teased me until I challenged all of them to enter. Guess what? None of them could manage it either. God bless those poor souls who had spent time in that place. Who knows what atrocities they experienced in there? Even now, 40 years later, thinking about that place still spooks me. Yikes.

I told Henry it would be my birthday that Thursday. He smiled and said we would have to celebrate. Now, 20 years ago, that would mean booze, girls, and a pile of Colombia's finest marching powder, if you get me. These days, maybe just maybe someone on the wing could make up some form of rudimentary birthday cake. Whatever. I stopped counting birthdays years ago. Meant little to me on the inside. I guess turning 50 was one of those landmark birthdays. No one cared about you turning 51 or 52, but 50, yeah, that was significant. When was the next one? I guess 75? Then 100? Who knew?

As we were closing up the metal shop that Wednesday evening, Henry teased me that he had some big plans in store for the next day. I think he was more excited than I was. God bless him. At least someone was enjoying themselves, eh?

I lay in my cell that night trying to fall asleep. As I tossed and turned in my bunk, my mind replayed different moments in my life, getting my first bike, learning to ride it, moving to New York City, riding with the boys, living like kings all through the 80s and 90s, moving to Arizona, starting again at age 40 with nothing, building myself back up from nothing, now here in Coyote Ridge Penitentiary, spending the rest of my days locked up. Damn. What a waste. I must have made every mistake there was to make in life. And yet others had done the right thing and been taken by cancer, killed before their time in a car wreck. Life really seems like a game of chance, Shoots and Ladders. One minute you're up, the next minute you're back at the start again. Some win, some lose. Some win for a while (like me), then lose. I was still here.

I had found my way. Henry had done this for me. I don't know why he had chosen me, but he had, and for that I was thankful. He had helped me find the right path, the path of construction and not destruction. To serve others. To do the right thing. Not destroy lives. Create. Build. Be useful.

Somewhere, long after lights out, I finally fell asleep.

I woke before the count the next morning. Despite the lack of sleep, I felt alright. So this is 50? When I was a kid, 50 seemed ancient. Somehow, I still felt the same as I did when I was 20. Okay, so my knees were shot. My right hip hurt like a motherfucker when it got cold. I had a little bit of a spare tire around my belly. I'm sure if I were still out in the free world drinking beers on the regular, it wouldn't be a small spare tire. What else? Oh, my hair was thinning. But other than that, I pretty much felt the same, the same guy, just a little grayer and a few wrinkles. Whatever.

Something was wrong. Our cells should be unlocked by now. Must have been a stabbing or a bashing last night. Of course, on the day of my birthday, two jackasses had to get in a fight and delay us getting breakfast. Bloody typical. An hour had passed. Nothing.

I sent a kite to my next-door neighbor, Brent. This one using a tiny piece of paper on a piece of thread. I fling it out from my cell. He retrieves it, reads my message, and then sends it back with a reply.

My kite said, "Hey, Brent. Do you know what is going on?"

I waited a few minutes. Nothing. Come on now. How long does it take to write "I don't know" or "This is what has happened"? I mean, seriously. Hurry the fuck up.

Finally, I heard the tap-tap-tap noise we had prearranged months ago as a signal.

I peeked out the crack between the floor and the door of my cell and spied my kite. Brent had replied. With a bit of effort, I retrieved it and reeled it back into my cell.

I grabbed the piece of paper and unfolded it. The note read:

"I heard someone on the ground floor had died."

Typical. As predicted, two dumbasses had gotten into it the night before my birthday. One had killed the other, and now, with an active investigation, we were forced to eat breakfast in our cells. No doubt the argument that got one of the cellies killed was over something dumb like, "What did you do with my flavor packet from my ramen noodles?" Small things could get you killed on the inside.

No breakfast came. Weird. Normally, during lockdown, we would get a tray brought to our cells.

Instead of stressing, I grabbed a book and jumped back onto my bunk. I wasn't going to stress it. Sooner or later, they would come for us.

Around 10 a.m. I heard my cell door go.

"Prisoner Raines, come with me," the guard instructed.

Weird, I wasn't being cuffed.

As we hit the ground floor, I noticed two paramedics milling about with a stretcher. Yep. Someone definitely got stabbed on the ground floor.

He led me out of C Wing towards the admin building. As we were exiting, I heard the familiar sound of the cells all being unlocked in unison. Lockdown was over.

I knew the path we were taking.

The Warden's office.

Why was I being brought here? I hadn't been in any trouble for a long time now.

"Sit here," commanded my escort, pointing to a bench outside the Warden's office. Again, I wasn't cuffed or chained.

Something was up.

The guard knocked on the Warden's door and entered.

I was alone in the corridor.

Chapter Thirty Four

Moments passed, and finally my guard reappeared.

"Raines, get up," he instructed me. I did as I was told.

The guard held the door open as I entered the warden's office. I was greeted by the sight of the warden, a doctor in a lab coat, and one other guard. What was he for? Just in case I lunged at the warden, I suppose.

"Have a seat, Prisoner Raines," the warden instructed. Again, I did as I was told.

The doctor started, "I assume you know the reason you have been brought here today?"

"No, sir, I do not," I replied.

The doctor looked at the warden, then back at me.

"Oh. Okay," he started. "I am very sorry. I regret to inform you that Prisoner Patterson has passed on."

I was confused. Who was Patterson, and why was he telling me this information?

"Um… okay," was all I could say.

"I know you were both very close," the doctor continued.

Close? I was beginning to think the doc had me mistaken for someone else.

I must have had a look of confusion on my face, because at that moment the warden spoke.

"John, he is trying to tell you. Your friend Henry… well, he died last night."

Henry? Dead?

"Wait. Henry is dead?" I asked.

"I'm sorry, John," said the doctor.

It slowly dawned on me. Patterson was Henry. I had never heard anyone use his last name before. Everyone referred to him as Henry, the guards and the prisoners alike.

"What… what happened?" I asked.

"Well, from what I can tell… a heart attack," said the doc. "We won't know 100 percent until after the autopsy."

"Oh," was all I could think to say. Was Henry dead? I think I was in shock.

"Well, if it's any consolation, he died peacefully in his sleep," said the warden.

That actually was a consolation for me. He didn't get stabbed or beaten to death by one of the younger inmates. That was something.

"Thanks. That is a consolation," I replied softly to the warden.

"Look, Henry didn't have any family," said the doc. "As per prison rules, we will bury him in the prison graveyard. Would you like to do the service?"

"Me?" I hadn't thought about his death or his burial. I had also never been to a proper funeral before. I had no clue what to say. I tried to think of some movies I had seen as reference points for how to behave.

"Sure. Thanks. I would like that," I replied.

"Very well then. Do you have any other questions for us?" asked the doctor.

"Um… when will the service be?" I asked.

"We have to complete the autopsy, then the funeral. So I would guess about one week. Okay?" the doctor replied.

"Ah… okay," I said.

The warden looked over at the doctor. "Raines, feel free to take the day off work today. You can start again tomorrow."

Work. I had totally forgotten about the metal shop. It would not be the same without Henry. Who was going to run it?

"Okay. Thank you, Warden," I replied.

"Oh, and one more thing, Raines," said the warden.

"What's that, sir?" I asked.

"Sargent Phelps says you have done incredible work in the last five years. He thinks you should become the new boss. Okay?"

Me? Really? Phelps put a word in for me?

"Oh… okay. Thank you, sir. I'll do my best to carry on Henry's legacy, sir," I said.

"Very good, Raines," said the warden. He then nodded at the guard who brought me into the office.

"Alright, Raines. Time to head back to your cell," said the guard.

I stood up and thanked the prison doctor and the warden before exiting the room.

I have to admit, I returned to C Wing in stunned silence. For nearly 10 years now, I have hung out and talked with Henry every day. Now he was gone. I was never going to talk to him again. I was at a loss. How could I carry on?

Chapter Thirty-Six

I started to fall back into old ways. I became very withdrawn. I felt like I no longer cared about anything. What was the point? That said, in a sense, I was kind of glad that Henry had passed on. Prison was no place for any man. But getting old in prison was the worst. You age faster inside, and you don't want to be old and frail in a place like this, where only the strong survive. Maybe it was a blessing for ol' Henry to die peacefully in his sleep rather than to spend another 20 years here with these thugs?

Regardless, I was aware that I was turning in on myself. I was enjoying my own company too much. I wasn't socializing with others. I just didn't care. I got up, ate food, went to work all day in the metal shop, came back, ate food, read a book in my cell, then went to bed. I did, however, carry on Henry's tradition of walking the rec yard every Saturday, lap after lap after lap. If nothing else, it was to keep his memory alive.

The service had to have been 10 days after Henry had passed. I wrote some words, and most of the guys on C Wing attended. You know, I always thought of funeral services as stupid and a waste of time. The person who died can't hear you, and all the crying from sad mothers and daughters was all for show. "Oh, look at me, I am so sad at my precious son's funeral," type of thing. A bunch of hysterics and drama over nothing.

With all that said, guess what? It actually helped. It was only now, at age 50, that I understood the importance of closure. One door closes, another door opens, the cycle of life, or whatever they call it. People told me afterwards that they liked what I had to say about Henry and appreciated me getting up to talk. So I guess that is something.

After the service, I returned to my cell to read. I was just moping about. I really couldn't even focus on the book I was reading. So I tossed it aside and tried to nap. I was halfway between asleep and awake when I heard Henry's voice in my head.

"Get up off your ass. Quit feeling sorry for yourself. Pick two apprentices and teach them everything you know. Pass down your knowledge. Give them a chance."

Fuck. That old bastard. Even in death, he spoke wisdom.

I jumped up out of my bunk and tried to refocus. He was right, of course. He had wasted time on me. He had shared his worldly knowledge with me. I had to pass it along. Maybe I couldn't be saved, but one of these younger guys could. He could get out by age 30. He would need real-world job skills to make money, to avoid coming back to a place like this. That's what I would do: pick two students and mentor them.

I made a list of all the young dudes in C Wing. Anyone gang-related or rowdy, I would avoid. I had no time for guys who wanted to fight, or worse, use the metal shop to craft weapons. Working there all day unsupervised was a privilege. First stabbing with a metal shank, and it would all be over, probably shut the shop down. Couldn't risk it. I crossed some names off my list.

I finally got it down to two names: Michael Bowen and Ken James. Much like Henry had shown up at my cell with two guards announcing I had been selected to work with him in the shop, I would do the same to Michael and Ken. Fuck it, why wait? I would go down there now and approach both of them.

Michael was sitting in his cell reading when I turned up. Hmm. Imagine that. Sounds familiar, right?

"Knock knock," I said, standing at his cell door. He looked up from his book.

"How's it going?" I asked.

"Yeah, alright. You're Raines, right?" he asked me.

"Yeah, John Raines. You mind if I come in?" I asked.

"Sure. Why not. I'm not doing anything," he replied.

I entered his cell and sat down.

"So, how long you got?" I asked.

"Ugh… forever," Michael replied. "Five fucking years."

"Five years is nothing, bro. You keep your nose clean, you'll be out in three years," I told him.

"Really?" he asked me.

"Yeah, I think so. You got anyone waiting for you on the outside?" I asked.

"Yeah. I got me maw and my girl," he explained.

"That's cool. Family is important," I told him.

"Yeah, I guess. Though I don't know how long my girl will wait for me," he said.

"Dude, trust me. If you have a plan for when you get out, she will wait," I said, trying to give him hope.

"You think?"

"Sure. The fact she hasn't dumped your ass already says something," I replied.

"Shit. I never thought of that," said Michael.

"What were you doing for work on the outside?" I asked.

"Video game store," said Michael. "It was alright."

"You can do better than that, man. If you want to support your girl when you get out, you gotta have a trade," I said.

"A trade? Like what? Be a plumber or an electrician? That costs money, bro," Michael replied.

"Any idea what welders get paid on the outside, bro?" I asked him.

"I dunno. A lot?" he said.

"Yeah, pretty much. Can write your own ticket," I said.

"Yeah, well, welding schools cost money. Money I don't have," he replied.

"Well, I run the metal shop for the prison. I will teach you if you want to learn," I explained.

"You would? Hang on then. What's the catch?" he asked suspiciously.

"No catch, man. Someone helped me out once, and I am passing it on," I said.

"I have your word that there is no catch?" said Michael, still not convinced.

"You have my word," I said, holding out my hand for him to shake.

He thought for a moment before grabbing it and shaking.

"Okay then. When do we start?" he asked.

So that was it. One apprentice. Now to recruit a second one.

Chapter Thirty-Seven

I said goodbye to Michael and headed two cells down to Ken's. I knocked, and Ken invited me in. Twenty-two years old, facing three years for assault charges. I never liked asking guys what they were in for, but from what other cons told me, it was some kind of barroom brawl that had gone wrong. I thought of all the bar fights I had been in throughout the 80s and early 90s, and at least then, very few places had security cameras. Then factor in assholes with these new smartphones. They can whip them out and start filming you. Next thing you know, you are looking at "Exhibit A" in a court case that will send you to prison. Things had changed, and not everything had changed for the best.

It didn't take me much to convince Ken to sign up as my second apprentice. He was a wannabe biker and could see the value in leaving prison in a couple of years with a trade under his belt, getting out, getting a job, making money, and starting to rebuild his life. That was smart. So many guys left, vowing never to come back. Well, guess what? Ninety-five percent of them always came back. Believe me, I understood. You get out, can't get a legit job because you don't have marketable skills, and you've got a criminal record. You fall back into what you know. It's easy money. It goes wrong, bing, bang, boom, you're back inside. Ken was determined not to make the same mistakes. Smart kid.

I met with both of them before breakfast the next morning. We grabbed a table together, and I explained to them how I would start them on basic welding techniques before teaching them metal fabrication. Both seemed enthusiastic students.

We headed over to the metal shop after breakfast. I had to admit it was weird to be in there without Henry. It was like his energy was still here with us in this place. He had spent so much of his life in this shop that it was almost like he'd imprinted his essence on it. Maybe that's what ghosts were, just the essence of someone who had spent so long in one location? Who knew?

I decided to do what Henry had done with me: set them both up on benches and have them work on their MIG welding. Exactly as I had done all those years ago, it made sense. It had worked for me. It should work for them.

Over time, it worked for Michael, but not Ken. In two years, Michael became a great welder. Ken, as much as he wanted to, was just terrible. He never graduated past the most rudimentary welds. Whether it was moving the torch too fast or not holding it at the optimum distance, he just could never do it right. At first, it frustrated the hell out of me. Then it came to me: not everyone is good at everything they try.

Turns out Ken was a great pinstriper. This was a field I didn't know much about, but given a chance and enough practice, Ken was a natural.

In time, their sentences were over. Michael got out first and quickly secured work as a welder. We worked locally, and as soon as his parole ended, he started working on oil rigs in Texas and Oklahoma, making great money.

Ken got out a year later, started working at a Kustom Kar shop, and was doing well. He got trained there on regular spray jobs and was making great money.

Both of them wrote to me when they could, and eventually, with a ton of money saved up, Michael returned to Phoenix, and the two of them opened their own shop. I was proud of them, and I was also kind of jealous to admit it. I had screwed up my own life so badly that I was still here, and they were out in the free world, thriving.

Oh well. No feeling sorry for myself. I got myself into this mess. I would have to get myself out of it. As the old-school criminals used to say: "If you can't do the time, don't do the crime." What more needed to be said?

So what now? I guess find another young, keen guy and train him up? What else was there? Looking back, at this point in my life, I had been behind the wire for a good 16 years. Would I be given a break? Would someone show leniency and reduce my sentence now?

For the next two months, I kept a close eye on all of the younger dudes on C Wing. In my opinion, there was no one there worthy of training. This current batch of guys seemed like a bunch of junkies who would rather get high than improve their situation. I spent months on my own, working on my own skills when not doing repairs for the prison. Better to be alone than waste time with someone who was just going to make your life a bigger mess than it already was.

Chapter Thirty-Eight

A year had passed. Most of the troublesome dudes on our wing either overdosed, got transferred to other wings, or made parole. Good riddance. None of them would be missed. They caused more problems being on the block than was necessary. There comes a time when no amount of drama and stress is worth being associated with a person, and these guys were the epitome of trouble. They would steal, lie, and cause fights. I was glad I never invited any of them into the metal shop. They would probably have gotten it shut down with their druggy shenanigans. No, thank you.

One day, we had a couple of transfers from other wings. One of those guys was a kid called Brian. He had been in A Wing, but had been transferred for beating up a convicted child molester. No matter where you went within the prison system, the one thing that all prisoners could agree on was the hatred of child molesters. Actually, thinking about it, most of the guards hated child molesters. There were many cases of guards "forgetting" to lock the cells of child molesters so that general population prisoners could "get at them" at night, usually resulting in an unexplained murder or two. No great loss, that was for sure. Anyone who interferes with a child shouldn't be in prison. They should receive the electric chair. No mercy for those monsters.

I started hanging out with Brian after work. He was a cool kid. At another time, in another life, we would probably have been friends on the outside too. Funny as fuck too. Very quick-witted. I decided to take a chance and offer him an apprenticeship in the metal shop. He was up for trying it out, too.

Guess what? It turns out that being a cool guy, a funny guy, someone fun to hang out with, doesn't necessarily mean you are going to be good at welding or metal fabrication. Not to be mean, but Brian was freaking useless! He had no natural ability whatsoever. He was a good dude though, and I had been alone in the shop for so long I decided to keep him on as a general assistant, sweeping floors, tidying up afterwards, a general dogsbody. He still earned his paltry wages for working, but it was more comedic relief than actual usefulness.

I did all the welding and metalwork required of us, and he kept me in stitches with his stories and jokes. Someone once said to me that "laughter was the best medicine," and looking back on it now, I hadn't laughed in so long. I'm talking, laughing so hard you can't see from crying type of laughter. That happened every day with Brian. He was like a court jester. Hilarious. I even encouraged him to go into stand-up comedy once he got out of here. He would have a killer career for sure.

So yeah. One day, I sent Brian out to get some measurements for a drain pipe that had been damaged during the monsoon season. You see, Arizona gets very, very hot in the summers, but we also get monsoons. Sometimes it would be like a month's worth of rain in one day. A lot of locals hated it, as it definitely made driving unsafe, but I found it a welcome relief from the relentless onslaught of blue skies and sunshine. Bizarrely, we rarely got actual rain in the winter, just during the summer. I think I could count only two winters in the last 16 years when it actually rained here. Crazy, right?

Brian returned with a piece of paper and my tape measure. He returned the tape measure to its designated spot (for which I was grateful) and laid the piece of paper on my workbench.

"You're not going to believe this," he said.

"Believe what?" I asked, assuming it was something to do with the storm-damaged drain pipe.

"You've got a mini me," he replied with a grin on his face.

"What?" I asked.

"You've got a mini me," he said again, still rocking his big smile.

I assumed, at this point, that I was being set up for one of his jokes, but I took the bait regardless.

"What's a mini me?" I asked.

"You've never seen *Austin Powers*?" he asked.

"Is that the comedy movie with that British guy?" I asked.

"Actually, I think he's Canadian," said Brian. "But yeah, that one."

"No, never seen it," I said.

"Well, anyway, the bad guy Dr Evil has a mini version of himself called Mini Me," Brian explained.

"Okay," I said, failing to see the punch line.

"So, you've got a mini me," said Brian.

"What are you talking about, brother?" I asked, starting to get frustrated with his story.

"We got a new guy. Just transferred onto the wing," Brian started. "Check this."

"Okay," I said.

"His name is also John Raines," said Brian.

"Huh. Weird," was all I could say. I didn't see that coming. To be honest, I always felt like the name they gave me for witness protection, "John Raines," sounded like a made-up name. Never in my wildest dreams did I ever think there would be a real guy named John Raines.

"Well, it gets even weirder," said Brian.

"Oh boy," I replied. "How does it get weirder?"

"Check this," said Brian, still smiling. "He's from upstate New York."

"No shit. Any idea where?" I asked. This was getting weirder.

"Uh, yeah, he told me… shit, let me think," said Brian. "Oh yeah, Rochester!"

"Oh, that's about a five-hour ride from me," I said. Well, it was about five hours from Wappinger Falls. That much I knew.

"Not only that," said Brian, "he's also a biker."

"Whoa! Really?" I asked.

"Yeah. Straight up," said Brian. "There's only one thing."

"What's that?" I asked.

"He's like 25 years younger than you," said Brian.

"Ahh," I replied.

What were the chances? A biker with the same name as mine and also from upstate New York? The universe had a strange way of messing with us at times. Or maybe we were really living in a simulation, as some modern-day physicists believed. Weird either way, though.

"I'll do you an intro at dinner time," said Brian.

"Okay, sounds good," I replied. "Let's get back to work."

I grabbed the sheet of paper with Brian's drainpipe dimensions and started figuring out what work I had for the afternoon.

Chapter Thirty-Nine

That night, at dinner, Brian spoke to the real John Raines and had him come to our table. He was at least 20 years younger than me, with a shaved head and a clean face. No biker beard, no goatee. He was also a cool dude for a younger guy. He and his buddies were bringing in coke over the border into Arizona from Mexico when he got caught. He managed to trick the cops into thinking he was alone, and his two pals got away. An honorable gesture for sure. For his troubles, he got 7 years. He was a long way from home and had no family to visit him. We immediately took him in as one of ours.

Turns out the real John Raines was good with a wrench, too. I guess years of working on your own bike will do that to a man. He had some basic metal-fabrication experience, and it didn't take him long to fit in with our little crew at the metal shop. He was a funny guy too, so he and Brian were like a comedy duo, constantly cracking each other and me up. I don't think I ever laughed so hard in my life as I did at this time.

One afternoon, we were working away on prepping some pipes for the laundry building. I guess they saw more wear and tear than most of the other workshops in the prison system. We were all very busy when a guard appeared at the door. Since I had the trust of the guards after years of being a "well-behaved little worker robot," they normally pretty much left us alone. I could count on one hand the number of times there had been impromptu visits by the guards since I had worked at the shop. Maybe twice? So I was quite surprised when this dude knocked and walked in.

"John Raines Senior. Can you come with me, please?" he said.

The younger John Raines looked at me and said, "That's you, ya old bastard."

"Thanks, kid," I said in reply, knowing he was just being a smart ass.

"You need me to cuff up?" I asked the guard.

He looked at me for a moment, then decided, "Nah. All good."

The guard led me back through C-wing and towards the admin building. I assumed we were going to visit the warden. I ran through a list of issues he might have with me, and the only thing I could think of was that there were two John Raines on the wing. Whatever.

"Where are we headed?" I asked.

"Warden's office," the guard replied.

Just as I figured.

We walked the now familiar corridors through the admin building to the warden's office. I took my assigned seat outside in the hallway as my escort knocked and entered. By now, he would be explaining that "Prisoner Raines" was outside and waiting.

It was probably no more than a five-minute wait before the guard reappeared and invited me in. Expecting a bunch of people staring back at me, I was surprised that it was only the warden and this one guard.

"Sit down, Prisoner Raines," said the warden, waving his arm at the chair across from his desk. I took the seat.

"How's your day going thus far?" he asked me.

"Good, thanks, Warden. Very busy," I replied.

"I've been hearing good things about you and the metal shop. Teaching the younger inmates a trade. That's very much appreciated," said the warden.

"Uh. You're welcome?" I replied.

The warden grabbed a file. He skimmed its contents and returned to looking at me.

"So as I said, it's come to my attention you have done a great job in the metal shop. Staff like Sargent Phelps have spoken highly of you," he continued.

"Okay," I said.

"It says here you have another 5 years on your sentence."

"I believe so," I replied.

"Well, I have just signed off for you to meet with the parole board at the beginning of next month. If all goes well, you might be out by the end of next month."

Early parole? I couldn't believe what I was hearing. It was like Henry had told me all those years ago. Do something good for Sargent Phelps, and you will be repaid down the road. I honestly gave up hope of ever getting out of here, and now I might be out by the end of next month? This was mind-blowing. I was at a loss for words.

I had so much to think about. Who should run the metal shop? Where would I stay? I assumed I would have to stay in Arizona until my parole was over. I could look for welding work. There had to be some places that would hire ex-cons. I was pretty sure there was still a shortage of talented welders out there in the free world. If that was true, a criminal record shouldn't be an issue.

Maybe I could reach out to Ken and Michael, see if they knew anyone who was hiring. Wow. This changed everything. Freedom? After all these years? Incredible.

I had done so many things wrong in my life. I had done my best to rectify these wrongs, and now the universe was repaying me by setting me free. Maybe there was justice in this world after all?

Whatever the warden said next to me, I don't remember. It was like his mouth was opening and closing, and I couldn't understand what language he was speaking.

Eventually, he got up and extended his hand for me to shake. I stood up and shook his hand.

All I could say was, "Thank you, Warden. I really appreciate this. I won't let you down."

"You've done well to rehabilitate yourself, Raines. Keep up the good work," was the last thing he said to me as I left his office with my security escort.

The walk back to the metal shop was a blur. I was giddy. I was on cloud nine. I could barely process what I had heard. I was leaving. I was getting out of here.

Brian and the real John Raines saw the expression on my face when I returned. Naturally, they asked me what was up, and I told them. They were super happy for me. True friends.

After the congratulations were over, I tried to get back to work. I had to cut and shape a piece of sheet metal into a drain pipe. I looked at the specs that Brian had drawn up earlier in the week, and they just didn't look right.

"Hey, Junior. Would you mind running back over to the laundry building and measuring up that drainpipe that needs replacing?" I asked.

"Hey! I already took care of that," said Brian.

"Did you?" I asked, holding up the piece of paper with all his specs on it.

Brian snatched the paper away from me and examined it.

"Oh. Okay. Ah. Well, never mind," he said out loud.

"Were you smoking crack that day?" I teased.

"You know I was!" joked Brian.

I handed the paper to Junior. "Yeah, so make sure when you come back it's not nonsense like this guy."

John Raines examined the piece of paper and looked over at Brian. "Drunk much?" he asked.

"Yeah. Yeah, get out of here," Brian replied, waving Junior off.

The real John Raines grabbed a tape measure from the wall and a pad and pencil.

"I should be back in 20 minutes," he explained.

"Cool," I replied.

Junior exited the building. I was about to turn around and get on with another job when I heard voices outside. I gestured to Brian to keep quiet.

I heard an unrecognizable voice and then Junior speaking. I couldn't make out exactly what he was saying, but I swear I heard "Stuey" and "Iron Dragons." Had my past finally caught up with me? Stuey, that prick. I knew even back then he was looking for me. Had it taken this long to find me?

I looked for a weapon. Something, anything. I grabbed a piece of steel pipe that could double as a baton and headed for the door.

Chapter Forty

I stuck my head out the door of the metal shop only to be greeted by the sight of three big dudes surrounding Junior.

I shouted out, "Hey, what are you doing?"

The one nearest me looked over and sized me up.

"Prison business. Get back to whatever you are doing in there," he said, trying to dismiss me.

"This is my business. Leave him alone," I said.

"Trust me. You don't want to get involved, old timer," said another of the three men.

"Nah. You don't want to get involved with him," I said, nodding towards Junior.

"Fuck off," said the first convict.

I gestured for Brian to step back. I moved the steel pipe in my right hand, so it wasn't clearly visible, and stepped out into the yard.

"This guy is one of mine," I said to the three newcomers. "Mess with him, you mess with me. Why don't you tell me what this is all about?"

The one who hadn't spoken sized me up, not spotting the steel pipe hidden in my right hand.

"This doesn't concern you, old man. Now walk away," he said.

"Can't do that," I replied. I caught Junior's eye. He looked scared. No, scratch that, terrified.

"So you defend rats now?" asked the third inmate.

"He's no rat. Now take a hike," I replied, prepping the steel pipe to crack some heads.

"You have no idea what you're messing with here, you old fart," said the first guy who had spoken to me.

"Let me guess," I said, looking all three of them in the eye, one at a time. "This has something to do with Stuey Latham and the Iron Dragons, right?"

"What?" said the criminal who just called me an old fart.

"You've got the wrong John Raines. You fools," I said. "I mean, think about it. He would have been what? Like, 5 years old back in the early 2000s."

The three thugs looked at each other, thoroughly confused. They were about to kill a guy who wasn't anywhere near the right age. How stupid can you be?

"Our intel is solid," said the third man. "He's here."

"Yeah, that's right. He is here," I readied my steel pipe. "He's not the guy you are looking for. It's me."

Before their dim-witted brains had a moment to process what I just told them, I charged with my steel pipe. Junior stepped back out of the way instinctively.

The inmate nearest to me barely had time to react before my steel pipe came down across his face. I was aiming for his head, but he just managed to take a small step backwards when I swung, causing the pipe to come down hard across his nose and not his skull. His nose exploded with a sickening crack, and blood went everywhere.

The prisoner nearest Junior grabbed him and started punching him. The inmate between Mr. Broken Nose and the guy wailing on Junior came at me. I swung out with the pipe, but missed. He managed to get hold of my right arm and tried to put me into some form of arm bar. I swung out with my left arm and connected with his temple. He let go with a yelp.

Meanwhile, the scumbag furthest from me was beating down Junior. That wasn't fair. This wasn't his beef. He just had the misfortune of sharing the same name as the one witness protection had assigned me. I had to get to him and help him out.

Mr. Arm Bar recovered quickly and lunged at me. We both hit the ground in a jumble of arms and legs. Somewhere in the melee, I lost grip of the steel pipe. I started punching Mr. Arm Bar's ribs repeatedly, trying to do some damage.

I managed to maneuver my body, so I had the upper hand on Mr. Arm Bar. My punches were definitely hurting him, but he was doing his best to lock in my left arm so I couldn't get back up again. Just as I was starting to tire, I felt a hard blow across the back of my head. Mr. Bloodied Broken Nose had rocked me badly. I could see Junior still going at it with the third inmate.

Gassing out fast, I shouted for Brian. Whether he heard me or not, I wasn't sure. I was tired and short of breath.

Mr. Bloodied Broken Nose started punching me, targeting my back and my arms. His punches weren't that hard, but they felt weird. The first one hurt a bunch. The rest? Just weird. I pushed with what little remaining strength I had to untangle myself from Mr. Arm Bar. I staggered to my feet to face Mr. Broken Nose, and there was blood all over the ground. I guess facial injuries bleed more than elsewhere on the body.

I swung a wild right that somehow connected with his jaw. He was wobbling on his feet when Mr. Arm Bar tackled me back to the ground. They both started in on me. I was gassing out. I tried to cover my head with my arms to protect what few brain cells I still had left. There was blood everywhere.

All of a sudden, I heard Brian yelling and then fighting one of my two assailants. I tried to roll out of the way of the remaining attacker, but my vision was going, and I found it hard to coordinate my arms and my legs. What the hell was wrong with me? I fell back into the dirt. The last thing I recall was Mr. Arm Bar taking a swinging kick to my head... then nothing.

Chapter Forty-One

I woke up in the hospital. Not even the pathetic prison hospital. A proper hospital. Of course, my left arm was handcuffed to the side of the hospital bed. It took me a moment to figure out where I was. I was in a lot of pain. Incredible pain. I looked over and realized that just in reach of my right hand was a buzzer-type device. Somewhere in my foggy brain, I realized that was the thing to call a nurse. I grabbed it and pushed the red button. Nothing. I tried again. Still nothing. I put my head back down on the pillow. Had anyone heard that?

Moments later, a nurse arrived.

"Ah, you're awake, Mister Raines," she said.

"Yes, and in a lot of pain. Can you give me something for it?" I asked.

She looked at me, then smiled. "You're already on the maximum level of morphine we are allowed to give you, sir."

It was then that I realized I was on a bunch of drips.

"Oh. What happened?" I asked.

"You were in a coma. You had swelling on the brain, and we also had to operate on you."

"Operate?" I asked.

"Yes, you had been stabbed about 50 times," she said. "It's a miracle you're still alive."

No wonder my entire body hurt so badly.

"Some of the wounds were infected, too. We had to clean those up, which is why you may feel a burning in parts of your body too," she explained.

Truth be told, I wasn't feeling much of my body at all. If they told me they had to remove both my legs, I would not have been aware; I was so out of it.

"How… how long have I been here?" I asked.

She grabbed my charts and did a quick calculation in her head.

"Six days," she replied.

Six days? What had happened to Brian and the real John Raines? Hopefully, both of them were okay.

"Do you know what happened to my friends?" I asked her.

"Friends? No, you came in alone," she explained. "Well, except for two prison officers."

"Okay. Thanks," I said.

"The doctor for your ward will be on duty in an hour. I will let him know you are awake," she said.

She checked all my fluids and the various machines I was strapped into and said her goodbyes. I just lay there with my thoughts. It hurt too much to move in any direction. I was pretty sure I had broken some ribs, too. At least with a broken arm or leg, they can put a cast on you. Broken ribs? There was not much they could do but tape you up and let time heal you. Everything hurt so bad. This sucked.

Chapter Forty-Two

You know, lying in bed and waiting for the doctor to turn up, I had nothing to do but reflect on my life. I had been a miserable human being. A gutless coward. I had dealt drugs. I had probably ruined lives. I had snitched on people who had called me brother. I had sent them to prison when I could have just let them be. I deserved eternal damnation for some of the things I had done. How did I end up like this? All I wanted to do was be free and ride my bike, and now this mess. I seemed to have torpedoed every relationship I had ever been in. I had no one to blame but myself.

Looking back now, I see stepping in and facing the real John Raines' attackers was the first step on the road to redeeming myself. Time to stop lying. Time to stop running. Time to face the music. I think a day comes for all of us when we have to face the music. Whether you want to call it karma or whatever, I don't care. I think you can't outrun your destiny. Who knows what happens after death? Maybe if you do bad things and never pay in this lifetime, you settle for eternal damnation. The things you think about when you are barely alive and tethered to a hospital bed, eh?

The weeks rolled by. I was finally starting to feel a bit better. I tell you, getting older, everything takes longer to heal. When I was in my 20s, I got into a bar fight, a busted lip, and some bad bruises. A week later, you're good to go. It had been nearly three weeks, according to my nurse, and I still wasn't even close to 100% healed up. It was going to take time.

One day, the warden came to visit me with a guy I didn't recognize. He told me once I was fully healed they were going to grant me parole, and this guy Rob Stevenson was going to be my parole officer. I would be free, but have to watch my step for the next four years. No screwing up. I was nearly 60 and starting again with pretty much nothing. No home ownership. No savings. No stocks invested.

Oh well. Screw it. I had faith I could rebuild my life. Let's face it, even the worst day in the so-called free world is better than your best day behind the wire. I was going to be free. I had a chance. I was determined not to screw it up this time.

Ian Harrison: It was at this time that I did my series of interviews with Jack Sullivan, or as he was known at this stage in his life, John Raines. We made plans to catch up a year after he was out of prison to see how he was doing. Who knows, maybe if there is enough interest, I'll do a follow-up series of interviews with him. Thanks for reading.

Thank You!

Hey, this is Alex. If you have made it this far, thank you! I hope you enjoyed the Wheels of Betrayal Trilogy. I am just finishing my follow-up to Fuel, Fire, and Freedom, a collection of Outlaw Biker Tales, which will be Book 2 of that series . Should be ready in a month or two, so keep an eye out for that one.

If you enjoyed Wheels of Betrayal Book Three, please consider leaving a review on Amazon, as that would greatly help me out.

Please also check out my novels on Amazon:
https://www.amazon.com/stores/AlexMcRae/author/B0F344WTHB

Also, feel free to follow me on Amazon here:
https://www.amazon.com/stores/AlexMcRae/author/B0F344WTHB

All for now

Alex

Arizona 2026

Extra special thanks to the following people:

Mooch, Tim at the Ton Magazine, Cary at Choppers Magazine, The Motorcycle Prophet, George Christie Jr, James 2, Hugo Dias, and Jeremy Rogers.

www.ingramcontent.com/pod-product-compliance
Lightning Source LLC
LaVergne TN
LVHW010702110826
845149LV00014B/3197

* 9 7 9 8 9 9 5 3 7 7 2 3 8 *